THE LION AND MISS LAMB

THE TRENGROUSE BALL
BOOK SIX

ELIZABETH LEYDIN

IMPROBABLE FICTIONS

ISBN 978-1-7635241-8-7

Improbable Fictions
PO Box 283
Annandale NSW 2038
Australia
contact@improbablefictions.com

*For Uma, whose wonderful writing
first introduced me to Tanjore's astonishing
history.
Many thanks for your help.*

THE TRENGROUSE BALL

The Trengrouse Ball…one magic night in a Cornish summer. Music, dancing, flirting and laughter. And deception, abduction, love and loss. New attractions, new hopes, and old flames rekindled. For some, a culmination. For others, a new beginning.

The Trengrouse Ball series follows the lives and loves of the Trengrouse family: eight grown children of the Earl of Trengrouse, each of whom is searching for the life they need; each battling their own fears but hoping for happy ever after.

After the Trengrouse Ball, their lives will never be the same again…

CHAPTER 1

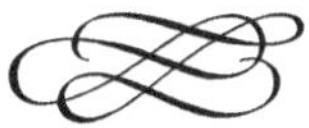

The name on the envelope was 'Miss Titania Lamb, care of the Duke St Orphanage'. Which was not her name, but it was for her none-the-less.

Sarah Lamb opened it slowly, sliding her fingers across the extremely expensive cream bond paper. A letter. For her. She'd never received an actual letter before, just one note from her last employer, firing her. The horrible woman hadn't even had the courage to say it to her face.

Matron Hutton peered over her shoulder. 'Who is it from?'

The address was written neatly at the top of the page. Mandeville House.

'From Mrs Mandeville?'

'Not exactly.'

They read it together.

Dear Miss Lamb

I have been informed that you are currently free to take up a post as governess to my twin five-year-old daughters, and that you are a trustworthy and intelligent young woman.

If you would be so kind, send a reply to this letter, indicating if you are interested in this appointment. If you are so inclined, I will send my carriage to collect you and your belongings tomorrow morning at nine of the clock. We shall discuss the terms of your employment then, but you will not find me ungenerous.

If you choose another path, I wish you all the best,

Lady Demelza Mandeville

· · ·

WHAT ON EARTH?

'How did she know about me?' Sarah looked at Matron in suspicion, but she held up her hands.

'Don't look at me, child! I've never even met Lady Demelza. Although I know is who she is. One of Earl Trengrouse's girls, as married John Mandeville from Gloucestershire.'

Matron reached automatically for Boyle's Court and Country Guide and opened it unerringly to Grosvenor Square. 'Yes. Here, Number 5A, between the Duke of Beaufort and the Marquis of Bath. Country seat, Mandeville House, Easthwaite, Gloucestershire.'

Good Lord. That was one of the best addresses in the city. The Mandevilles must be very wealthy. Who on Earth had talked about her to Lady Demelza?

Matron plunked a piece of letter paper in front of her with an inkwell and quill.

'You answer that right now!'

Yes indeed. She was in no case to quibble over not knowing her employer or worry she might be going into a difficult house-hold. Matron had been kind enough as it was, letting her come back to Duke Street until she found her feet, which was against all the Orphanage regulations.

Dear Lady Demelza,

I am delighted to accept your offer of employment.

I shall be ready at nine of the clock tomorrow.

Your faithful servant,
Miss Titania Lamb
PS Please note that I have not ever used my birth name. I am known as Miss Sarah Lamb.

'You can't write that!' Matron said, shocked.

'I certainly can. I'll take a job on sight unseen, because I must, but I will *not* be known as Titania!'

'You've always been headstrong.' Shaking

her head, Matron went to give the reply to the waiting footman.

She had employment. Relief swamped her; she gripped the table to stop her head swimming as the dread let go of her heart. Without a good character from her last employer, she'd given up hope of a respectable governessing position. Being a chambermaid was the best she could expect. The worst was beyond thinking about.

Her bag. She would pack her bag, and be ready to meet her new employer. Matron came back, dusting her hands with satisfaction. She'd really been very kind.

'Matron? How old is Lady Demelza?'

Tilting her head as she always did when considering numbers, Matron hesitated. 'Twenty-seven, mebbe?'

Only three years older than herself. That was good. It meant there'd be no grown-up sons to moon over her and get her dismissed.

She got up, swinging Matron around in a dance.

'I have employment!'

'Give over, do!'

Sarah laughed. A new start. Perhaps this was the turning point she'd needed for so long.

THE TWINS WERE GOING to start squirming any moment now. Sarah couldn't blame them; sitting still while they waited for the funeral party to come back to Mandeville House was a dull business for her, let alone for two six-year-olds.

She met Lady Demelza's eyes, and her employer nodded, so she got up and held out her hands to the twins.

'Adelia, Grace, come with me and we'll find you some milk and perhaps an apple.'

They jumped up immediately, clearly relieved to escape the mourning atmosphere. The shades were drawn, of course, and their mother was motionless, while the female Mandeville relations—most of them barely acquainted with the girls—spoke quietly and cried.

It must be so hard for the twins. Their father, just gone. Three days after contracting an ague when he was chilled by a sudden rain while fishing. It had been a dull, cold day, as well, for late June. This English climate could never be trusted from one day to another.

Everything sudden. His illness. His death.

They had no sons, and of course the estate was entailed, so this might be one of the last nights in their own home before they were suddenly required to move.

She blinked back her own tears and smiled at them as they took her hands.

'You've been very well-mannered, girls. I'm impressed.'

Preening, Adelia said, 'We want Papa to be proud of us.'

Grace, following along as she always did, nodded. 'He liked it when we were well behaved.'

Of course he did. What father did not?

Well, she couldn't speak to that from personal experience, but it stood to reason.

They went into the kitchen where the girls were made a great fuss of. Cook pressed a cup of tea into her own hands with an abjuration to 'Drink it, it'll do you good.'

She sat and let the kitchen staff keep the girls amused.

Where would they all live? The old fear of being homeless rose up to hiss at her, but that was ridiculous. Lady Demelza Mandeville wasn't going to be poor, even if she was a widow.

If the worse came to worst, her employer would go home and live with her family in Cornwall.

Whether she'd still need Sarah then…she shivered. This was nonsense! Even if they already had a governess in Cornwall, Lady Demelza would give her an excellent character and help her to find employment. She was a *true* lady. Yet it was hard to beat back the fear which had followed her all her life.

·   ·   ·

ENDELLION TRENGROUSE CAME into the kitchen to let the staff know the men had returned from John Mandeville's graveside.

Melza's two girls were sitting at the kitchen table, and next to them...

It was as though he'd been given a leveller. Hard to catch his breath.

Brown hair with auburn lights in it. Beautiful. A perfect profile. Skin smooth with a soft rose in the cheek. But her expression was bleak.

House of mourning, Lion. She's not going to be grinning at two girls who've just lost their father.

He was possessed of a piercing desire to see her smile. To have her look at him.

She turned her head. Grey eyes. As beautiful in full face as in profile. Zounds! What a woman!

Who *was* she?

'Uncle Lion!' Adelia jumped up from her chait and ran to him, burying her face in his coat.

'Is Uncle Felix here too?' Grace asked.

When he nodded, she ran out towards the hall, Adelia following her.

The Aphrodite rose and spoke in an apologetic tone. 'It's no use trying to make them behave when Mr Trengrouse is around. He's so good to them.' Her voice was musical, and quiet.

Say something, man.

'Felix is a good lad.' Yes, make yourself sound like an old man. He bowed. 'I don't think I've had the pleasure. I'm Endellion Trengrouse—but everyone calls me Lion.'

She curtseyed. 'Miss Sarah Lamb, Mr Trengrouse. I'm the girls' governess.'

Of course she was. That's why he hadn't met her before at Mandeville House; she'd have been in the schoolroom, and he wasn't as attentive an uncle as Felix. For a bare second he considered the social gap between them, then threw the thought away. She was infinitely above him: her character shone in her bearing, her manner, her voice. A lady.

He stood back to allow her to precede him to the hall. What curves! Aphrodite was never so beautiful. Just as well he hadn't said that out loud; that goddess was jealous of the beauty of others. He might have brought a curse down on them both.

The good—the *wonderful*—thing, was that he knew where to find Miss Sarah Lamb. All he had to do was be a dutiful uncle and brother.

Not that he resented that. Poor Melza would need them all now she had to leave Mandeville House.

WELL! Sarah drew in deep, quiet breaths. *Calm youself, girl.* Calm, hah! When a sun-god walks into your kitchen, you're entitled to be a little overset.

Good Lord, he was handsome! So tall. Surely well over six foot. And with that mane of blond hair barely contained by po-made, no wonder they called him Lion.

He'd hardly spoken to her, but he had been polite, which was not always the case. Men of his class seemed to think that all governesses were desperate for attention. The wrong kind of attention.

The gathering in the drawing room was suitably subdued, although the food was good and the coffee excellent. Sarah withdrew to the edge of the room, ready to take the girls back to the schoolroom when Lady Demelza gave the sign. She tried not to look at the sun-god standing with her employer, and she failed utterly.

MANDEVILLE'S COUSIN GEORGE, a small, mousy man, greeted him with a manner which nicely drew the distinction between a relative and the heir apparent. Not a bad fellow, but what a shame he had to turf Melza out! His wife, who was sitting next to Melza, was a different kettle of fish, and would no doubt be puffing herself up in her own conceit already, before John's body was properly cold.

Melza came over to them and drew both

him and Mandeville aside. 'A word, Mr Mandeville?'

'Of course.' He was surprised; it wasn't quite *done* to be talking about what came next at the wake. They followed her to John's office. It still smelt of the cigarillos he'd liked.

Demelza stood in front of the desk. She didn't even ask them to sit down. Something was up. It wasn't like Melza to be odd.

'Cousin, I have some news you may not wish to hear,' she said. She placed a hand over her abdomen. 'I am expecting John's child.'

Lion whistled internally. That would set the cat among the pigeons! George Mandeville, to do him credit, rallied from the blow immediately.

'Then we shall go on as we are until the birth,' he said.

'If Lion agrees.'

Of course, he was one of the executors. The solicitor was the other, but he'd follow

Lion's lead. He clapped Mandeville on the shoulder.

'George is quite right.' Mandeville looked pleased with his approval. 'I'll explain things to Mrs Mandeville.' The man positively lit up at that; no doubt he'd have dreaded that exchange. 'Is there anything we can do, Melza?' Lion added.

'The steward is quite competent,' she said. 'I think he'll be able to keep the estate functioning well until…until we know more.'

Until she had a boy or a girl. A boy, and she stayed here for life and hired an estate manager. A girl, and at the best she'd be off to the dower house. For a while, until that shrew married to George pushed her out. There was no chance she'd want a stunner like Demelza around her sons, who were both gormless idiots and had been gazing at her with—well, probably with the same expression with which he'd looked at Miss Lamb. Just as well Mama hadn't brought Melissa or Kerenza; they'd never have caught their breath.

They were all alike, the Trengrouse girls: dark beauties with deep brown eyes and porcelain skin. His brothers, too, were dark-haired. Only he was fair.

That was an old scar; he pushed away the twinge the thought gave him. Might as well bite the bullet and face the old harpy now.

'Into the fray, Mandeville,' he said, following Melza out of the room.

This changed his plans. He'd thought he'd have time here, sorting out John's affairs, but if the whole place was in limbo, he'd get the work done in no more than a day, and no excuse to stay. No excuse to linger with the governess.

Just as well Melza had promised to come to Kerenza's birthday ball next month.

CHAPTER 2

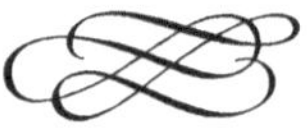

They arrived at Trengrouse Hall two weeks before the ball. There was already a governess, Mrs Siddons, a widow. She had taken the opportunity of Sarah arriving to take a visit to her grown son, who had just had a baby.

So here she was, with not two little girls but five children altogether. Locryn, Viscount St Swain, the eldest Trengrouse son, had a ten-year-old boy, Jory, named after his father's father, the current earl. And there was an eight-year-old boy, Jamie, named after his mother's father the duke, and a four-year-old girl, Rosalie, named after no one that she could discover.

They were nice children, but *loud*.

Since it was summer, lessons were light and most of their time was spent in the gardens, playing rounders or climbing trees. It was delightful to be in the Cornish sun; how she loved the warmth! The orphanage had been cold all year round, being stuck between two tall buildings; in winter it had been icy, no matter how many clothes they were bundled into. She could never get enough of being warm.

Her employer had given the girls permission to climb trees.

'We all did it,' Lady Demelza had told her, a trace of amusement in her sad eyes. 'Let them run a little wild. Just don't let the big boys tempt the girls into anything dangerous. Collecting tadpoles is fine, but don't let them go after birds' eggs—the earl has forbidden it.'

Governessing wasn't a life she loved; but on this fine summer's day, wearing a big straw hat Lady Trengrouse had insisted she take, sitting on a blanket on the South Lawn while young Jory instructed Grace and Adelia in the finer points of batsmanship, she was happy.

Besides, she had a new frock on: one of Lady Demelza's light-coloured dresses which she couldn't wear during her mourning. 'And by the time she's out of blacks and greys,' Tancred, her lady's maid, had told Sarah, 'these will be right out of fashion.' Oddly, the maid hadn't objected to Sarah having the dresses and pelisses and even a riding habit, although traditionally maids were given their lady's cast-offs to sell or re-purpose. Sarah strongly suspected she'd been compensated by Lady Demelza, but it would have been the height of ingratitude to ask.

So today she was in a lovely pale blue muslin with blue ribands, and felt not at all ashamed to be seen by the family.

'Uncle Lion!' Rosalie shrieked. Immediately the game was forgotten and the children swarmed Mr Trengrouse.

Do not blush. Do *not.* Don't even look at him!

Of course she had to look at him. He was grinning at her, clearly inviting her sympathy as Jamie scrambled up to sit on his shoulders, and Jory and Adelia swung on each arm, talking incessantly.

She got up and curtseyed. He tried to bow, but it was impossible.

'Leave your uncle be, children,' she said. 'Adelia! Jory! Jamie, come down from there!'.

Endellion Trengrouse laughed and swung Jamie to the ground.

'They're doing no harm. In fact, I wondered if they'd like to go for a buggy ride to the sea.'

'Yes! Yes! Yes!' the chorus went up. As one, they turned to her.

'*Please*, Miss Lamb!' Jory begged.

'Miss Lamb wouldn't be so mean as to say "no"', Adelia assured him.

'Wouldn't I?' She sighed. 'I suppose I wouldn't.'

They cheered, 'Huzzah!'

'You must all wear hats. Go and find them.'

They raced off and Mr Trengrouse walked over to her. 'It's a big buggy, a double seater. You're most welcome to come.'

An image of walking along a Cornish beach flashed into her mind. Dangerous, to spend *any* time with him. She was already far too aware of him; standing this close, his scent of horses and leather and male was quite heady. It would be sensible to say no, and to have a quiet afternoon by herself for once.

Restlessness rose up in her, stronger than ever, a wild desire to be anything but sensible. To run and shout and laugh and have *more* out of life. It was a reprehensible thing in a governess.

She couldn't bear to be sensible one second longer.

'Thank you, I'd like that,' she said. His face lit up, grey eyes shining with genuine delight.

A shiver went straight through her, from

head to toe. She was a fool, undoubtedly a fool.

LION HADN'T BEEN sure she'd come. It had hung in the balance for a moment; he could see the indecision in her eyes, although it didn't show on her face.

How had he known? He'd never been able to read anyone as he read this woman. As though they were attuned on some deep level.

Romantic poppycock.

As he sorted the children into the seats of the buggy so that Miss Lamb would have to sit next to him, he pondered it. Romantic, perhaps. But not poppycock. He handed her up into the buggy. Every movement, every glance, every breath held meaning for him, as though Plato had been right, and they were two halves of the same body.

It shook him.

Lion climbed up into the buggy and the

stable boy let the horses go and jumped up behind. The children cheered.

'Reminds me of our governess taking us to the beach,' he said. 'That's what this buggy was made for, and why it's so big. Eight of us.'

'Your poor governess!' she said, smiling. 'She must have been quite frazzled.'

'Mama wasn't so cruel. We had two teachers. A governess for the girls and a tutor for the boys. They swapped some of the lessons as we got older, so we all learned Latin *and* watercolours.'

He'd loved painting. Funny, he'd forgotten that—painting wasn't an occupation for a Trengrouse man and God knows he'd have been bullied mercilessly at school if he'd stuck to watercolours.

'That's very progressive.'

'It was Melissa's idea, when she was about four. She adored the classics and felt it was absurd that knowledge should be quarantined by one's sex.'

'At four?'

'Oh, yes. She's a prodigy, you know.'

He should enlist Melissa's help to get some time alone with Miss Lamb. She, of all his sisters, wouldn't care about social class. Although she wasn't the most maternal girl. He couldn't expect her to take the children off their hands. Still, she'd come up with something. She always did.

He smiled at Miss Lamb and was ridiculously thrilled when she smiled back.

HE HAD HANDED her up into the 'buggy' as if she had been a lady.

Sarah wasn't used to such consideration, and it unsettled her. So silly. He'd clearly been raised with impeccable manners, that was all. She held her own in the sporadic conversation, and had to smile at the thought of Endellion Trengrouse painting dainty watercolours.

They followed a well-worn track toward the sea. It dipped down into a protected dell of full-leafed beech trees, green shade flickering over them. Then they turned a corner, went down a little further, and there it was.

The stable boy jumped down to the horses' heads, and the children scrambled out and ran, already bare-footed, onto the yellow sand. She sat, frozen by awe.

Of course she'd *read* about the ocean. But…

It was a fine day, with a brisk breeze, and the aquamarine waves were edged with white lace. White horses, did they call it? The colour deepened further out from shore. Deeper. It must be deeper there.

And the scent of salt and something else she'd never smelt before…invigorating.

'Are you coming down?'

Startled, she looked at Mr Trengrouse, who was standing at the side of the buggy with his hand out to her, waiting.

'I'm so sorry!'

She slid down, steadied by his hand in hers, but she simply nodded and kept staring. The movement. The heat. The *beauty*.

'Miss Lamb?' He had offered her his arm.

Good Lord, gentlemen didn't do that to the governess!

She was shaken enough by the sight of the sea to take it. They walked out, following a kind of trail of rocks, over loose sand and down to near the water's edge, where the damp sand was darker and firmer.

The sound. Hiss, and slap and an occasional crash from a larger wave.

The children were running wild, screaming with excitement. She should look after them, not dally here. Her heart expanded in her chest; she was dizzy with the sheer *size* of the blue carpet which stretched to the horizon. Being able to see that far was both entirely uplifting and profoundly unnatural for a girl raised in the centre of London.

'Are you all right, Miss Lamb?'

'Oh, yes!' she said impulsively. 'It's so…so *big*!' Exultation. That was the name for this feeling.

He laughed, but not unkindly. 'Your first

time by the sea? It is extraordinary. I never tire of it.'

'How could you?'

They stared at each other with a moment of perfect understanding.

What was she thinking? Feeling the blush move up her cheeks, she turned away from him to watch after the children.

It wasn't so large a beach, after all. They had reached the tumbled grey boulders at the end and were racing back. Adelia, as always, in the front. They were fine.

'This is a, a cove? Is that right?'

'Yes. Hall Cove, they call it around here, although I doubt it's even named on any map.' He looked down at her with a mixture of amusement and admiration. Dangerous, that look. She'd seen it before; it was often a prelude to some amorous advance.

Not in front of the children. He wouldn't.

He didn't. He offered her his arm again, and they walked out onto the damp sand to meet the children. Sarah was thankful she'd worn old half boots to go into the garden. They'd take no harm here.

Adelia reached them first and grabbed Sarah's hand. 'Come, Miss Lamb, it's the *best* way to run!'

'Adelia!' she remonstrated, but Mr Trengrouse laughed and slid his hand into hers

'Yes, come on!'

He and Adelia took off, and she perforce ran with them. Her hat flew off, she almost stumbled, the wind was whipping her face with spray and salt, she was definitely *not* acting like a lady…

She'd never been so happy in her life.

Lion showed her how to build a sandcastle.

By then, she'd given up pretending to be sober and cautious.

'Your sister did say I could let them run wild,' she'd said, with a question in her voice.

'Lord yes!' He grinned at her. 'We all did. It's good for them. Come, I'll show you my favourite thing to do at the Cove.'

There'd been a blanket in the buggy; he laid it out for her to sit near the low water mark, and showed her how to build a castle.

It wasn't long before she'd taken off her gloves and joined in, and then the babies came too, and all of them constructed a truly magnificent structure, with shell windows and turrets and a moat.

The sun had moved towards the west, though it would be hours before dark. Time to get the babies home.

'Hungry, anyone?' he asked.

Miss Lamb stood up, brushing sand off the children and herself. He pushed down an impulse to ask her to brush him off too; one touch of her hand, and he suspected he'd make an exhibition of himself in front of the children.

'*I'm* hungry,' Adelia said.

'So am I!' agreed Grace.

'Teatime!' the others chorused.

They trooped up to the buggy, and found Jol, the stable boy, asleep in the shade of a sea-buckthorn. Lion toed him awake, not unkindly.

'Up and at 'em, lad!'

As they drove home, Miss Lamb, still slightly sandy, beside him, Lion was hit by an image of how it could be, driving their own children home from Hall Cove one day. But looking down at her, at her firm mouth, and silent attention to the children, he realised that, for the first time ever, he had no idea what a woman thought of him.

She'd not flirted once. Not given him a single glance of encouragement.

Yes, she'd taken his hand as they ran. She'd made a castle with him. But had it meant any more than her running with Adelia? He might as well have been another of her charges for all the *awareness* she'd shown of him.

Except for that one moment, when she'd stared into his eyes, and blushed.

He'd hold onto that.

When he was ten, his Uncle Moxham had given him his first rifle, and taken him and his older brothers out duck hunting on an inland lake.

The key, his uncle said, was patience.

He liked duck hunting. Unlike fox hunting, which he abhorred. That was all about neck-or-nothing speed and following a pack of blasted hounds as though it *meant* something.

But duck hunting…you sat in the cool clear air of dawn, and simply waited. Oddly, Locryn, who was supposedly the stolid one, just couldn't do it, and was sent back to the horses sooner or later for fidgetting. Petroc had stood his ground and followed orders, like the soldier he would become. Endellion had loved it.

The cool grey light before dawn. The mist on the lake, the sound of the ducks' wings, whirring in the air, the sense of being outside his normal, heavily controlled school life…he hardly even took a shot, but those were some of his best memories.

Miss Lamb's eyes were the same grey as that magical dawn light.

He could be patient for her.

Patient and canny.

SHE WOULD PUT this day into the special drawer in her memory and keep it for when she felt despondent.

Otherwise, she must not think of it again. It would be too easy to let her awareness of Endellion Trengrouse grow into something much more dangerous.

No matter how gentlemanlike he acted towards her, she was not a lady, and not in his sphere.

She bit her lip, remembering that line from Lady Demelza's offer of employment; *a trustworthy and intelligent young woman* it had said. Not *a trustworthy and intelligent young lady*. Because she was a servant. She couldn't afford to forget that, not for a second, no matter how her heart stirred when Mr Trengrouse took her hand.

When the buggy stopped in the stable-yard, she jumped down and reached up for

Rosalie, who was drooping with tiredness, before Mr Trengrouse could come around to help her.

Rosalie put her head down on Sarah's shoulder and wrapped her little legs around her waist. She was a shield between Sarah and Mr Trengrouse, a warm and loving little shield.

'Say thank you to your uncle, children,' she said.

'Thank you, Uncle Lion!' they chorused immediately, shifting from foot to foot like a single creature.

'Wash your hands, and then you may ask Cook for tea.'

'Huzzah!'

Mr Trengrouse was laughing. 'Lord, they remind me of us as children!'

Another difference between them. She couldn't imagine being so light-hearted as a child. From the very beginning, it had been impressed upon them all that life was hard and their lives, in particular, were precarious.

'You've had a blessed life,' she said.

Her words arrested him. He stared down at her, no longer laughing, his eyes thoughtful.

'Yes. I suppose I have.' His eyes flicked up to the dark stone of the Hall. 'In some ways, very blessed. But no one has a perfect life. Not even a Trengrouse.' His beautiful mouth twisted awry and he turned away abruptly, and then turned back as if compelled.

'Thank you for accompanying us, Miss Lamb. It was a delightful afternoon.'

He bowed and walked off and she watched him go, astonished. That was what *she* should have said. Had he been mocking her?

His voice had *sounded* sincere…

Unsure but suddenly certain she'd misunderstood *everything* that had happened, everything he had said and done, she followed the children to the back door.

It would be wise of her to avoid spending any more time with Mr Endellion Trengrouse.

That way lay heartbreak.

CHAPTER 3

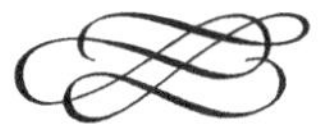

'Look, Miss Lamb!' Adelia and Grace ran into the schoolroom, each brandishing something.

'Girls! Ladies do not run! Especially inside the house.'

'Sorry, Miss Lamb,' Grace said. Adelia brushed away Sarah's words and thrust a white shape at her.

'*Look,* Miss Lamb! See what Grandmama has given us. One each!'

It was a toy lamb. About six inches long and four or five tall, with a coat of actual lambskin, and a calico face, skillfully embroidered with eyes, nose and mouth. The eyes even had eyelashes.

Cold swept down through Sarah's whole body. Dizzy, she reached for the back of a chair to steady herself.

'See, Miss Lamb?' Grace said. 'I have one too. Grandmama *made* them. Made them her*self*!'

'Because she loves us,' Adelia said complacently. 'Even though Father is gone, we do have lots of people who love us, don't we?'

That brought Sarah's attention back, and she hugged both of them.

'Yes, of course you do. You're very lucky to have such a big, loving family.'

The girls nodded wisely and sat down on the settle to play.

'We shall be shepherdesses!' Adelia said.

Sarah watched them numbly. It couldn't be. But it could. She went to the nursery door and called Becky, Rosalie's nursemaid. Rosalie was asleep. Becky could watch the girls for a few moments.

'Yes'm,' Becky said, and put her stool where she could watch both rooms.

It would be foolish of her. It would be *unwise* of her. But those lambs…she couldn't help herself.

As she went towards her bedroom, her steps quickened. Into the small room. To her portmanteau. To the compartment at the bottom, which she rarely opened. She looked closely. Yes. Yes.

Snatching the contents up, she walked far too quickly to the stairs and ran down them.

At this time of the day, the countess would be in the small study off the morning room, doing her accounts. Sarah had come to know the pattern of the Trengrouse day over the past week. She'd memorised where each person normally was, to reduce the chance that she'd accidentally meet Endellion.

The study door was ajar, but there were no voices within. Breathing erratically, she knocked and went in without waiting for an answer.

The countess, beautiful and perfectly groomed as always, looked up in surprise from a ledger.

'Miss Lamb.'

Wordlessly, Sarah thrust out her hands. The countess frowned and leaned forward, examining the once-white little bundle. Then her face cleared.

'Ah, you kept it! How nice.'

Nice? *Nice?*

'It was you.'

The countess blinked up at her, and gestured for her to take a seat. Good. Her legs were wobbly.

'My dear Titania-'

'No one calls me that! They call me Sarah. Sarah Lamb, because when I arrived at Duke St I wouldn't let go of it.'

'I remember.' Lady Trengrouse sighed. 'I'd made it for Demelza – I gave all the girls one when they were six. I finished it waiting for your mother to... you needed it more. I made Melza another one.'

Sarah's heart was beating in huge, hard thumps. Her fingers were cold.

'It was you. You were the woman who took me away from my father.'

'My dear! No such thing.' The countess looked horrified. 'Your father was in no state to look after you. He'd caught the consumption himself by that stage, and only had weeks to live. He wrote me, begging me to look after your mother and you, because he could no longer get out of bed. So I went to see...' She paused, her gaze becoming distant. 'Your mother had very little time when I got there. She was decently housed, of course, and had servants, but they weren't much use. You were trying so hard to help...'

She remembered. Not much, but her mother's gasping voice saying, 'I love you, Tania,', and a woman's kind blue eyes...she'd felt such relief when she'd realised that the woman—*this* woman—was going to take charge. The gift of the toy lamb had been a lifeline, promising safety, and she'd grabbed it and held on.

Then felt such betrayal, such terror, when she'd been carried out to the countess's carriage, and driven away from everything she'd ever known.

'I'm so glad you were able to say goodbye, my dear,' Lady Trengrouse said gently. 'Once she was gone, I needed to get you to somewhere you'd be looked after.'

'Gone? She was gone when you—when we left?'

The countess laid a hand over hers, which were still clutching Lamb.

'She died almost as soon as I arrived. As though she'd been waiting for someone to come and take care of you. I promised her I would. And I have.'

Anger coursed through her, and her fingertips tingled with it. 'You left me at Duke St.'

'It was so lucky that I remembered! I was leaving for Cornwall the next day.' For the first time, she looked uncomfortable. 'Duke St was...frankly, it was set up to look after the natural children of gentlemen, so it seemed ideal.'

'Of course.' Her tone was bitter, but she didn't care. She remembered those first few days at Duke St. All the strange children, the noise, not knowing how to act, what to say.

The terror of being among strangers, of being dumped like an unwanted puppy.

'Well, my dear, your father was dying. His heir has never shown the slightest interest in family matters. I *would* have had you here, but my husband…' Lady Trengrouse let her voice trail off, but Sarah understood. The earl hadn't wanted his children tainted by a bastard.

'Two things,' Sarah said. She must keep herself under control. No screaming. No shouting. No blame. Her employment depended on it.

'Yes, my dear?' The 'my dear' was in a much cooler tone this time.

'Who was my father? And what did you mean, you'd looked after me?'

As though surprised by the questions, the

countess got up hastily and went to the window, gazing out onto the lawn beyond.

'Your father was my cousin, the Duke of Langwick.' A *duke*? The children at the orphanage had often whispered that they were all by-blows of the nobility, but a *duke*? She clutched Lamb tighter.

The countess took in a deep breath. 'I cannot believe that woman didn't tell you. I expressly gave orders that you should be informed of your origins on your majority.'

'I was employed by the Fentons at that time,' Sarah said. 'A school with ten students. I had very little time to visit Duke Street.'

'Still, Mrs Forbes could have *written* to you.' This was the countess being displeased, and her tone froze Sarah where she sat.

'Mrs Forbes died when I was sixteen. Mrs Hutton is the Matron now.'

Like a bird settling its feathers, the countess calmed down, and sat again.

'Unfortunate. I had thought—I gave instructions that you be informed of your family, and that I was willing to give you whatever details you wished about your father. He loved you very dearly, you know. When I heard nothing, I assumed you had decided on a clean break. Which, truthfully, may have been best.'

'You said you–'

'Looked after you?' For the first time, Lady Trengrouse showed some discomfort. 'Well, in some ways.' Her mouth pinched. 'I know it should have been the new duke who bore that burden, but Hereward has always been a care-for-nobody. So I arranged that you be raised with the accomplishments of a lady. So that you could have employment as a governess. It seemed the most…suitable career. Far more suitable than your mother's choice of opera singer.'

The music lessons. The watercolour lessons. The Latin tutors. The geography and history lessons. Some of the other children had attended, so she'd never realised they were all for *her*. And the clothes. She had always had slightly nicer clothes than the other girls…but only slightly.

'That was you?'

Lady Trengrouse looked down, as if embarrassed. 'Your father was my cousin, you see. I was very fond of him. It seemed the best solution.'

As if she were a messy problem which needed tidying away.

'And then, of course, I organised your employment in the parlour school, and your first governessing role with Mrs Youngville. Silly woman! She should have kept that stepson of hers far away from you. What did she *expect* would happen?'

In a minute, she could leave and then take some time to sort all this out so she didn't feel quite so head-over-ears.

'And my employment with Lady Demelza?'

'Well, of course. So fortuitous! The girls were just the right age to have a governess and there you were, at liberty, so to speak.' As though the mention of the twins had set all to rights, the countess patted her hands again. 'And there's no need to be concerned about what will happen once they're grown. Demelza and I have agreed that you will make an excellent companion for her once they have left the nest.'

'Th-thank you.'

'Of course, Demelza won't tell them of their…connection to you.'

'Of course not.'

Complacent, the countess leaned back and picked up her quill. Clearly, Sarah was dismissed.

'I shall look forward to telling you more about your father at some other time,' Lady Trengrouse murmured, and then looked up. 'Endellion favours my side of the family, so that will give you a very good idea of what he looked like.'

They were cousins. She felt sick. She wanted to rave and rant, but she rose, keeping her composure, and dropped a curtsey.

'Thank you, Lady Trengrouse.'

The countess nodded absently as she totted up a column of figures.

Sarah went out quietly. Up the stairs quietly. Into her room.

She put the lamb back in its compartment, letting it go reluctantly. She couldn't let the twins—let *anyone*—see it. Because their *connection* wasn't being acknowledged. She wasn't a poor relation. She was just the governess.

The floor was hard, but she couldn't make herself get up. She pushed the portmanteau back under the bed and leaned her forehead against the cool counterpane. Emotions whirled and collided within her.

Gratitude: the Trengrouses had paid for every advantage she'd ever had. Made her current life possible. Allowed her some dignity so that she wasn't forced onto the streets or into a manufactory or mine, like most orphan girls were.

Rage: they'd organised her life to suit themselves. How *dare* they! How dare *that woman* think she had the right to pick and choose her employment, her way of life, how much she should know about her own family. Her own *mother*!

Relief: she would never have to feel the terror again. That soul-destroying fear of being abandoned, alone, unwanted and poor. She was safe. For the first time in her life, she was safe. As long as she gave satisfaction, she had a job for life, in the most luxurious of circumstances. A pretty cage.

Desolation: the only family she had didn't want her. Had never wanted her. The Duke of Langwick was a darling of the newspapers: rich, care-for-nobody, just as the countess had said. Her uncle. And the countess was her first cousin once removed. Endellion and his siblings were her second cousins. But never to be acknowledged.

Of course not.

The feelings swirled and rose and fell until she was dizzy, but she couldn't cry. Rage, gratitude, relief, desolation merged into one thing: a stone-cold determination never to show any of them how she felt. She would be the perfect lady; and a lady never showed her true feelings in public.

Three deep breaths. There. She rose to her feet, adjusted her hair back to its normal smooth bun, and went back to the schoolroom, where, as if no time had passed, as if her world hadn't completely rearranged itself, the twins were still playing shepherdesses and Becky was sitting on her stool mending one of Rosalie's stockings.

'Thank you, Becky,' she said calmly. 'Girls, you can play shepherdesses in the garden if you wish.'

'Huzzah!' Adelia said. 'The boys have gone to find tadpoles. Can *we* catch tadpoles, Miss Lamb?'

At least she didn't have to make a decision. 'Certainly,' she said. 'Your mother has given permission.'

The lambs were left abandoned on the floor. Sarah couldn't help but pick them up and tuck them safely on a cushion before she followed the girls out, choking back a sigh as she did so. Her poor mother. Dying with no one but a stranger present, knowing that the man she'd adored was dying too.

Her knees were still wobbling as she walked down the stairs, but by the time they reached the garden, she was herself again.

Trying to go to sleep that night, she suddenly heard the countess' voice say, 'He loved you very much, you know,' and grief pierced her chest like a sword, doubling her over. She sobbed into the pillow, using every trick she'd learnt in the orphanage to cry silently, so no one would know her pain.

CHAPTER 4

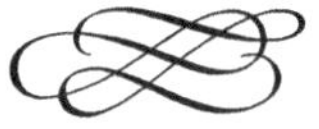

$\mathcal{M}$iss Lamb was avoiding him.

He was certain of it. Endellion searched through the ground floor apartments. Not in the library, not in the morning room, not in the courtyard, nor on the terrace.

The first week Melza and the girls had been here, he'd seen her several times—in the garden, on the terrace, at breakfast once, around the house. And of course that wonderful afternoon at the cove. Now…nothing.

They had only three days until the ball, and after that he was going back to London, to meet his Indian shipping partner. That appointment couldn't be changed. He had only three, perhaps four days to-

To do what? Fix his interest with her?

Yes.

He stood stock-still at the edge of the terrace, surprised by his own intensity. She was just a woman. And a governess. Not someone his family would approve of.

Hah. As if he cared for that. He'd stopped caring what his family—well, what his *parents*—thought when he'd first worked out why he felt as though he didn't belong. His brothers and sisters were dear to him, but none of them were bosom bows. Felix came closest. He'd be a good person to talk this over with, but he was off at the tin mine most of the day, being an engineer.

Lion leant against the stone balustrade, newly installed only last year, and stared unseeingly at the smooth lawn and the gardener who was carefully raking up the droppings of the sheep which had shorn it so smooth this morning. His mother, as always, had everything ticking away like clockwork.

Ignoring the twist in his stomach that the thought of his mother always gave him, he set himself to solve the puzzle. Why would Miss Lamb be avoiding him?

Could someone—could his *mother*—have warned her off?

Oh, that was entirely possible, which made it imperative for him to find her.

The nursery first.

He was in luck. The nursery door was ajar, and voices sounded inside. *Her* voice. How could he know it so well, when he'd heard her speak so rarely? But that tone, that soft, smooth, golden tone, was unmistakable.

Time to play the doting uncle—which really wasn't so hard. The girls were poppets, and Locryn's brood reminded him of his own childhood. Besides, those girls were coping with their father's death, and deserved a little coddling.

He pushed the door open a little, and his heart clenched. Miss Lamb was sitting in the rocking chair, with one of the twins in her lap, the girl's head on her shoulder. Grace, he thought; she had tears on her little face. They were slowly rocking. Sad, but such a beautiful sight. The sun came in from the far window and lit Miss Lamb's auburn hair with a halo. She could have been a Da Vinci Madonna.

Hesitating, he almost left.

'Uncle Lion!' That was Adelia. She sprang up from next to the rocking chair, and flung herself at him. He swung her up until her head was on his shoulder, as Grace's was on Miss Lamb. Poor little thing.

Miss Lamb met his eyes. 'They're missing their father.' He was surprised that she'd say it so bluntly, but the girls nodded in unison and both clung more closely. How he wished his own parents had been as honest with him!

He rocked Adelia and patted her back, until she let out a huge sigh and squirmed out of his hold. Immediately, Grace jumped up from the rocking chair and the two of them raced out of the door to the school-room next door where, he realised, the other children were playing something quite noisy.

Miss Lamb rose collectedly, her face showing nothing.

'Thank you.'

Clearly a dismissal, but bedamned with that! If she could be blunt, so could he.

'You're avoiding me.'

She blinked in surprise, but otherwise her expression didn't change.

'Yes.' He hadn't expected that. His heart beat too fast, and his palms were sweaty, as if he were some pimpled youth with his first sweetheart.

Only the pimples were missing.

'Why?'

The faintest smile (or was it a sneer?) twisted her mouth. 'It's not appropriate for the governess to spend time with the son of the house. I assure you, nothing good can come of it for either of us.' He was about to argue with her, when she added, 'Especially for me.'

'Melza wouldn't-'

She levelled a calm gaze at him. 'All I have, Mr Trengrouse, is my education and my reputation. Without reputation, my skills mean nothing. There is nothing so easy to taint as a woman's reputation. Deservedly or not.'

She was right. Damn the world to cinders, of course she was right. But not if he— if his intentions were *honourable*.

'Not if I'm courting you.'

That gave her an actual physical jolt, as if he'd pushed her. 'Don't be ridiculous.' Her voice was sharp.

'I'm serious.'

Abruptly, the calm left her face. She flamed into magnificent anger.

'Well you *shouldn't* be! How impossible, how *juvenile*, to think you could court *me*!'

'I don't see why I shouldn't.' He could feel his face set into the stubborn lines his father so hated. 'I…I feel that we would do charmingly together.'

'*Charmingly*?' She choked on a laugh. 'Oh, Mr Trengrouse, you have no idea-'

A step forward, and he could reach for her hand. 'No one could say a word against you if we were-'

Her soft hand evaded his; her fingers came up to close his lips. She smelt of some herb: chamomile? The touch left him dumbstruck.

'Don't say it. It's not possible. I-I'm flattered, but you have *no* idea.' Grey eyes beseeched him. 'Oh, I have to tell you. But you must swear to keep it secret.'

A secret. Another man, probably. His whole body seemed to grow heavy in an instant. He nodded against her hand, and she took a deep, fortifying breath.

'I'm…I'm illegitimate. Both my parents are dead. I have no family.'

Stepping back, lowering her hand, she raised her chin as if in defiance. As though she knew she'd dealt him a body blow.

A by-blow. Born on the wrong side of the blanket. The baton sinister.

'I-'

The girls ran back in and each grabbed one of Miss Lamb's hands. 'Come and see! The dog has had *puppies*! Jory says we can go and look!'

They dragged her out without giving her a chance to say no. He'd seen her with them before, however. If she'd wanted to, she could have stayed. No doubt she'd left rather than face his mumbling, bumbling excuses, his backing away.

Illegitimate.

Did he care?

He'd be a hypocrite if he did, given his own parentage.

Could he despoil the Trengrouse name by marrying a bastard?

Just watch him.

SARAH HAD no idea what he'd thought. How he'd reacted. He'd gone so still.

Why was she even thinking about it? No gentleman would ever marry a bastard.

It just wasn't possible. That bright, shining moment where he'd said he wanted to court her was a mirage. Illusion. The reality was this: she was a governess, and would be for years, and then she would be a companion to Lady Demelza for the rest of her days, living in her house and eating her food, having to be grateful for the least little consideration.

If she were *lucky*. If not, the old terror of being on the street, alone and beggared.

With an effort, she dragged her attention back to puppies and small girls.

It was something, though, to have Endellion Trengrouse even *thinking* about marrying a governess. He must, at the least, really have a *tendre* for her.

Something to keep her warm in the lonely nights.

CHAPTER 5

Lady Demelza had taken it into her head to spend the night of the ball with her daughters. She couldn't attend herself, being in deep mourning, and perhaps she was feeling the absence of her husband.

The girls curled up on either side of their mother with satisfied faces, and demanded a story. Sarah didn't offer to stay; it was clear she wasn't wanted.

She hesitated as she closed the schoolroom door behind her. Music drifted up the staircase: a country-dance. Her toe started tapping involuntarily. She avoided music usually, except for the pianoforte. It had such an *effect* on her, which Matron always blamed on her mother's blood. Matron was right. Mother and music went together like light and shade: where there was one, there was the other. Humming, singing, playing guitar, practising scales every day...her mother had moved in a cloud of music. It was one of the few things Sarah could remember.

An opera singer, the countess had said. She hadn't known that before, but it made perfect sense. Dispiriting, in one way. Theatre and opera were notoriously full of the demi-mondaine, at best, and the completely dissolute, at worst. She couldn't believe her mother had been so steeped in sin; but what did she know?

It wasn't worth worrying about now. She had all the respectability she would ever have, and it was up to her to keep it. Yet she did love music so, and tonight she was dressed in one of Lady Demelza's ball gowns, a silk in old gold…she could pretend, at least, that she was fit for the ball.

She hung over the stairrail, but the orchestra was still faint.

It wouldn't hurt if she went down a little way, would it? Just to where she could hear better.

Creeping down the staircase, keeping to the shadows as best she could, she tried to hear. There wasn't anywhere in the old house, except perhaps the dining room, where she could hear perfectly, and the supper was set out in there.

She could go outside…

It was an outrageous idea, but the dance ended, and then began again: a lively reel. The tune fizzed in her blood like champagne. She *had* to get closer.

Doubling back, she went down the servants' stair and slid out sideways into the passage to the garden door at the bottom. The sound was clearer here, and she tripped lightly out the door, heading for the lawn at the west side, where there were doors from the ballroom. The windows were wide open on this glorious moonlit night, and the music poured out like wine, heady and intoxicating.

Inside, couples swirled and turned, bright silks and dark coats, gleaming jewels and broad shoulders, smiles and laughter. Like one of the folktales she read to the children, where ordinary people caught a glimpse of Fairyland.

Fairyland was dangerous for mortals, and should be avoided, lest the poor human never be satisfied with ordinary life again.

The reel ended. Sighing, she turned away. Best to go back and read in her room. Better, darn her stockings. Something mundane and decidedly ordinary, to bring her back to Earth.

She rounded the end of the building, planning to go right around the house and come to the garden door that way.

Endellion was there, in the dining room, piling little cakes on a plate. Sarah froze. A chance to look at him. To drink him in, without embarrassment or shame.

A deep part of her heart twisted. In evening clothes, he seemed more distant than usual. His hair tamed, his posture perfect. He smiled at the maid behind the table and held out the plate for more.

It was a very bad idea, this mooning over Endellion Trengrouse.

He turned, as if to go through to the other room, to the hall, instead of going back to the ballroom, and stared straight into her eyes.

He couldn't see her, surely? She was in shadow. He *did* see her. Hurriedly, he put the plate down and made for the side entrance, nearest the dining room, which had been the old front door, centuries ago.

She picked up her skirts and ran. She didn't know why, just that her heart was bounding like a hunted fox, and she knew that, if he caught her, nothing would ever be safe again.

Footsteps behind her. Would the big

front door be open? Perhaps she could nip in there…

Her feet hit the gravel drive with crunching sounds, and more crunches followed her. She had a chance, just a chance. If she could get away, disaster might be averted.

'Sarah!' He wasn't even winded, the pig! A few more strides, and his hand landed on her arm, pulling her around to meet him. She almost fell, but he steadied her. 'Sarah, don't! Don't run.'

His eyes, full of *something* she'd never seen before, were fixed on her pleadingly, his face sculpted by moonlight and his mouth tender, and she had no chance at all. Disaster crashed over her.

'Don't run from me,' he said again.

Behind them, the music started up. A waltz. He slid his hand down her arm and took her hand, leading her to the opposite side of the drive, onto the South Lawn, where their steps were quieted by grass.

'Dance with me.'

Such a dangerous thing to do. He raised her hand to his lips and kissed her knuckles. Her bare skin. A shudder went right through her.

She'd tried so *hard* to be a respectable woman, but she was her mother's daughter, after all.

When he drew her into his arms, she went willingly. Her last charges, the Youngville girls, had had a dancing master, and she had stayed for all their lessons as a chaperone. She knew the steps of a waltz *theoretically,* but she had never danced it.

That didn't seem to matter. She fitted into his arms as if by design, and he held her firmly. Her mother's musical instinct did the rest, so that she followed him as lightly as one of the inhabitants of Fairyland.

He was so *big.* Tall and strong and solid as a tree; but graceful as a tree in the wind. They didn't speak, just looked at one another and moved as one.

This wasn't happiness, as she had felt on the beach. This was something quieter, and deeper, and more *real*. She *belonged* here, in his arms, as she'd never belonged anywhere before. But this was all she'd have, because they could never marry. It would ruin him. He had to be made to see that.

Lion gazed into Sarah's eyes and *knew* that this was it. His life would never be the same. He'd defy the whole world to have her as his wife. Bedamned to the lot of them!

Never in his life had he felt so right.

The music died away and they came to a stop near the corner of the front.

'Sarah-'

She put up a quick hand to stop his lips, as she'd done once before. This time, he caught her hand and kissed the palm passionately.

'You know this is the end of it,' she said breathlessly. Good. This feeling wasn't all one way. Couldn't be.

'I don't care-'

'You *think* you don't care-'

'I *know* I don't care! So you're-you're illegitimate. My business partners won't even blink. All they care about is profit. And they're the only ones I care about. My family can go hang if they cut us off.'

They wouldn't. Not really. Papa would be furious, but he didn't really *care* about anything Lion did. The rest...they'd come around. Even Locryn, eventually. Family first, and damn everything else, that was the Trengrouse way.

'There's something you don't know,' she said breathlessly. She gave his hand a shake. '*Listen.* You have to know this. I'm your cousin.'

'I beg your pardon?'

Of all the things she could have said, that was the least expected.

'My father...' she faltered, but he squeezed her hand, suddenly protective, and she went on. 'My father was your mother's cousin. The Duke of Langwick.'

He gasped as though he'd been drenched

with ice water. Cold shot from his heart through every limb.

No.

'No. That's not-'

'Your mother told me. We're second cousins. So whatever you think can happen between us, can't happen. It would all come out. My parentage. The Duke St orphanage. My mother the opera singer. Can you imagine the scandal?'

He took a step back and dropped her hand. No.

No.

His *sister*? Could that be why she seemed so familiar, immediately?

Surely not. He shook his head.

'So you see,' she said, her voice breaking a little. 'It's doubly hard. It would taint the children, you marrying a nobody, but to marry your own cousin's bastard—it would destroy your family's standing.'

She didn't know. That was something. She didn't know what horrendous mistake they'd almost made. He'd almost *kissed* her.

'Yes.' It was all he could manage. His vision of a happy life together, a *joyous* life, smashed into pieces around him.

'So you see.'

'Yes.' He should say something else, but he couldn't.

'Well.' She stepped back, and gave a small curtsey. 'Thank you for the dance. I-I enjoyed it.' Tears in her eyes, but what could he do, or say?

There was nothing which could save them. Better if she never found out the truth.

In the face of his silence, she turned and ran, light-footed, across the grass and onto the side path.

She'd get back all right.

A carriage passed him on the drive. Out of habit, he looked: Denzell Kelynack's coach. Poor little Katie had been looking peaky earlier; perhaps Den was taking her home.

Yes, that was the way. Fill his head with meaningless drivel, and *don't* think about the fact that he was in love with his half-sister.

The very thought made him sick to his stomach.

THE LOOK ON HIS FACE!

She might as well have said that she was a leper's daughter!

Safe in her room, Sarah sat on the bed and breathed. It was hard to do. Everytime she thought about that look, her breath hitched and turned into a sob, but she would *not* cry. She wouldn't.

One didn't. The world was hard. Her life was never going to be like the life the Trengrouse women lived. He would never marry her. He'd probably have never married her even if she *hadn't* been his cousin's daughter. It was just a summer madness that his family would have talked him out of.

Probably.

In any case, it was done now. That look… as though she'd thrown dung at him, or something even worse.

He would never want to dance with her again.

He was safe. His reputation, the girls' reputation, *her family's* reputation, was safe.

Oddly, that was comforting. She might not be an open member of it, but she could still do the Trengrouses a service no one else could do.

She could save Lion from himself, and she had.

A sob escaped her lips. She snatched up a pillow and smothered the sound.

She needed a new plan.

Instead of tamely accepting that she would live with Lady Demelza for all her born days, she could *do* something instead.

Save her pay. Demelza was quite generous. Save enough to buy a little cottage, where she could give pianoforte and singing lessons. Be her own mistress.

It might take a while (*years*, a voice deep in her mind said), but it could be done.

She could set her sights on that, and put away any memories of Endellion Trengrouse forever. There was no need for a governess to ever see the brother of her mistress, and if she did, well, one would be…polite. Polite and distant.

Ruthlessly polite.

That was a good word, ruthlessly.

Ruthlessly, she pushed down the pain and the panic, and let the pillow drop.

It had always been a mirage, the idea of her and Endellion. She let it evaporate like morning dew.

All she had to do was keep breathing.

CHAPTER 6

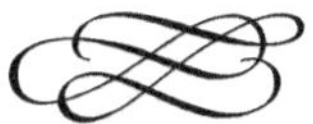

The whole house was in an uproar over Ives' and Katie Kelynack's marriage and Petroc's betrothal, but be-damned to the lot of them. What did he care if Ives had compromised Katie? They were a good match anyway; they'd probably have realised it in a year or so. And Petroc and Beatrice had been smelling of April and May all week, so he had no idea why anyone was surprised.

He was heading to London as soon as possible. He had to get away from any chance of seeing *her* again.

Briefly congratulating both the newly-emerged couples, he said goodbye to his parents, gave Melza's girls a hug, collected his valet and gear, and left before nuncheon.

London. Business. Something to concentrate on, that's what he needed.

Thank God Avi Arasan, his Indian business partner was arriving soon. He would bring an avalanche of work, and Lion could bury himself in it until he stopped shuddering at what he'd almost done.

How could it be, that he'd wanted her so? It didn't make any sense at all. Surely there should have been some warning from his blood?

Staring resolutely out the carriage window, he concentrated on passing fields, villages, towns. He would not think about her.

He would *not*.

It was good that there were so many children for her to manage. The days were full of activities, nature walks, games, even some lessons on rainy afternoons.

The nights were harder.

Once the children were asleep, Sarah sat in the chair by her bed, staring out the window, trying to darn her stockings or finish a chemise she was making, and failing to set a stitch for hours at a time.

She wasn't even thinking of him, not really. It was more that, without the stimulus of the children's demands, her brain slowed and stopped, like a clock with a missing pendulum.

She just stared.

Sometimes, when the candle guttered and she came back to herself, there were tear marks on her dress; but she didn't remember crying.

In the end, she had to discuss it with *someone*, and there was only one possible person. She gathered her courage and followed her employer out of the girls' bedroom after they'd been tucked in.

'My lady..'

'Yes, Miss Lamb?'

There was no easy way to say this.

'I know who my father was, Lady Demelza. The countess told me.'

Oddly, her employer looked relieved at this news.

'Oh, thank goodness. I've never known whether to discuss it with you…Mama didn't tell me all that much. And for Heaven's sake, call me Melza. We *are* cousins.'

'I wanted to thank you for-for taking a risk on me. If anyone knew my situation, it might redound badly on the twins.'

Lady Demelza—Melza…no, that was just too informal. Demelza—waved that away. 'I think our credit is good enough to avoid anything like that.'

How nice. How *nice* to be so well placed in the world that ordinary considerations just didn't apply.

A FEW DAYS after the ball, after all the guests had left, Lady Demelza invited her to dine with the family and then sit in the parlour after dinner. A nod to her now-acknowledged cousinly connection? Perhaps, although she *had* often sat with the Mandevilles in the past.

Sarah wanted to refuse, but it was for the best. She would have to stay alert, and not cry, and not think of Endellion. Much for the best, really, even if those evening conversations were trying. The family were so *nice* to her, and their very niceness emphasised the social gap between them.

In the end, she offered to play the pianoforte for the company, and after that it was easier; she was relegated to the background, incidental music, while the family's life went on around her and plans were made for Petroc's wedding.

Lady Beatrice, his new fiancée, was very kind to her, giving her music she'd had brought from her own nearby home.

'For you're far more talented than I shall ever be,' she said. Very kind, with understanding eyes.

Seeing Lady Beatrice with Petroc was like a knife in her side; they were so happy, so clearly in love. Sarah watched them as she played, even though she knew it was stupid. *That* was what love looked like: equals, together in public, claiming each other.

She gazed long and hard at them, memorising all the things she would never have. The touch of a hand, a secret smile, a caught breath.

Cut them out of your mind, she told herself. They are not for you.

It was a relief when Lady Demelza told her that they would be going back to Mandeville House at the end of the week.

London, and business, helped. As did the iron discipline which Endellion had cultivated at a very young age; from when he had realised that his father treated him differently to his other sons.

Avi Arasan arrived from Tanjore on a wind-swept, rainy Thursday, and stayed with Lion only a few days before looking to buy his own house.

'My wife wants to bring the children to London in a year or so,' he explained, 'to make sure their English is good enough before Kavin goes to Harrow.'

His own English was immaculate; he was a Harrow alumnus too. It was where he and Lion had become friends. The slender, intelligent Avi had been a natural target for bullies when he'd first arrived. Lion had tried to defend him, but Avi would have none of it. He was a natural boxer, and soon taught the others to respect his fists.

Up until then, Lion had depended on his size and his strength in fisticuffs, but Avi showed him science. Even Gentleman Jackson had commented favourably upon their form, when the two of them had, as senior students, dared to attend Jackson's saloon during the holidays.

Avi and Lion had planned their import-export business during their years at school, and then university, and then when Lion worked for Avi's family company in Tanjore. Avi was the son of one of the princes of Tanjore, and had access to considerable family money. And Lion…going over the latest profits with Avi, he reflected that the inheritance he'd once wanted to reject had been well invested in their first ship.

Now, they owned a fleet, and the trade in Indian muslin and ceramics, spices and tea, had made them both extremely rich.

They were still the best of friends, too. Although sometimes that was inconvenient.

'You're not looking well,' Avi said to him, as they toured houses for sale in Mayfair.

'It's nothing.'

'You looking hag-ridden isn't nothing.'

Lion shrugged. 'An affair of the heart.'

Kindly, Avi let it drop, but a few weeks in, he brought it up again, after dinner in his new, luxurious, fully-furnished house. It had been amazing how Indian money could overcome the reluctance of Lord Parslon to sell to a 'native'.

'This affair of the heart,' Avi said, sipping

his port. 'It must have been serious. You're still looking thunderous.'

Perhaps it was the port. Perhaps it was the kindness in Avi's eyes. Or perhaps it was the knowledge that Avi himself was a natural-born son. It meant nothing in Tanjore; his mother had been a well-respected concubine to the king's brother, and his status, therefore, was secure. He wasn't in line to inherit his father's title but, other than that, he was just as respected and respectable as his legitimate half-brothers.

Lion poured out the story.

'But if this girl is your cousin—your second cousin, you say?—then why may you not marry?'

'Because she's *not* my cousin.' He'd never said it out loud. Never admitted it to anyone. He could trust Avi, though. 'My real father is *her* father.'

Avi blinked and sat up straight.

'You're sure?'

How he wished he wasn't.

'I'm the only Trengrouse male in seven generations to have fair hair.'

Avi waved that off. 'It happens so, sometimes. A freak of the blood, do they call it? My cousin looks more Danish than Tamil, thanks to a Danish trader who married a great-great-aunt.'

'The Duke—my mother's cousin—when he died, he left me an inheritance. I was only a child, and they told me it was because he was my godfather. But…' Lion's throat closed up, remembering the day. He coughed, and went on. 'I received the inheritance on my majority.'

'I remember,' Avi said. 'We bought the *Shamrock* with part of it.'

'Yes. The other part was a manor in Devonshire. The only part of his estate which wasn't entailed.'

'Still, he *was* your godfather. And he died early, didn't he? He had no other children.'

The image of Sarah sprang up in his mind, bright and vivid. His breath caught. 'No *legitimate* children. Only Sarah.'

'Ah.' Leaning back, Avi fixed his dark eyes on Lion. 'What aren't you saying? I remember, at the time, you seemed…angry. But I didn't like to pry.'

'I appreciated that.' He took a drink. 'When I received all the papers, there was a copy of the will. It said that he was leaving Otterling House to me because, and I quote, "of my paternal care for him".'

Avi straightened up fully and thumped his glass onto the table. 'Zounds!'

'Exactly.' There. It was out. The words that had been festering ever since he'd first seen them.

The words that meant he could never, *never*, think of Sarah as anything more than Melza's governess.

Pouring him another glass, Avi nodded. 'It is hard to read that any other way. There's a slim chance…'

'Slim to none.' Lion sighed. 'No. I'm…I'm not illegitimate, because that's not how the law works, but I am misbegotten. I accepted it. It's only because of Sarah that I've even *thought* about it since then.'

'You're still angry.'

'That my mother was—unchaste? Yes. Wouldn't you be?'

Too late, he remembered that Avi's mother would be considered no better than a lightskirt by London Society, and winced. Avi laughed, and then sobered.

'My mother might not have been chaste by English standards, but she never betrayed my father. Nor ever would.'

That was the source of his anger. Betrayal. Betrayal of his father, which became a betrayal of *him,* leaving him out of the circle of his father's love, of what should have been his right to paternal affection.

Bah! It was childish, to maunder on about it. Over and done with.

'Well,' Avi said. 'Perhaps you can find yourself another nice girl. Introduce me to London Society. In a few leyars, I'll have two girls to bring out, and I'd prefer to be well established before then.'

That was surprising. 'You want them to marry Englishmen?'

'I do. India…there will be uprisings and tribulations from now until forever. We see the signs even in Tanjore that the British are bringing change to all of India. I want my girls to be well established here, where it's safe.'

'They will…they'll meet a great deal of… resistance.'

'They'll be looked down upon, yes,' Avi agreed. 'But they will also have extremely large dowries. And they're beautiful girls. I don't expect to have to fight off their admirers, but I *do* expect them to be creditably established.'

'Of course, anything I can do…'

Avi smiled brilliantly. 'I'm afraid, my friend, that I will need you to open doors for me, so that by the time they arrive, the sight of a brown face in the room will be an accustomed one.'

'The Season hasn't started yet, but when it does, you can count on me.'

Even if going to ball after ball would bore him silly. Perhaps he *could* find someone who stirred his blood as Sarah did.

It wasn't impossible, no matter what his heart said.

THE TALK with Avi stirred up something else; the realisation that his father the duke had not provided for Sarah. Which seemed…odd.

Lion went back and examined *that* will; it was dated five years before the duke's death; before Sarah's birth, no doubt.

Well, that explained it—although surely the man knew he was dying? He should have made provision. No use asking the current duke. Hereward was a—the politest term was 'care-for-nobody', but Lion was more inclined to call him a selfish oaf.

But *he*… He had a whole manor which, rightly, should have gone to Sarah.

He understood her enough to know that she wouldn't want him to make it over to her, but with a little finesse he could make life easier for her.

She didn't even have to know it was him.

CHAPTER 7

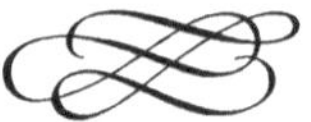

GLOUCESTERSHIRE

The long drive back to Mandeville House was welcome. It allowed Sarah a pause; time to regather herself into the old shape, the old state of mind she'd once enjoyed.

That almost worked.

Once she was back, though, she feel easily into the accustomed patterns of life, even if she had odd, restless dreams night after night.

Lady Demelza was showing her pregnancy now, and was increasingly motherly towards the twins, involving them in preparing the baby's nursery.

'Although of course, it might not *be* the baby's nursery,' she said in an aside to Sarah. 'If it's a girl, the nursery will be in the dower house.' Demelza made a face. 'Or in London. I'm not sure if I can live with the new chatelaine.'

Mrs Mandeville had visited several times, assessing each room with avaricious eyes. Sarah could see why living so close might be unpleasant.

Ridiculous that her heart leapt at the thought of living in London, where her employer's brother might more easily visit. Ridiculous and stupid. He'd cut her off without a word. Seeing him would only twist the knife.

She tried very hard to settle back into normal life, but in the mornings, her pillow would be wet with tears she had wept in her dreams.

. . .

'So, it can be done?' Lion gazed expectantly at Mr Lodge, the Duke of Langwick's solicitor.

Mr Lodge, a bluff, hearty kind of chap, pursed his lips and nodded.

'Yes. The fact that she has, as it might be said, been "discovered" by your family again after some years is most fortunate. We might even say that it *is* the true story. Although I do not quite understand why you want her to believe it comes from the duke.'

'She's a young lady with a great sense of honour. I believe she would accept from the head of the family what she would *not* accept from anyone else.'

Mr Lodge nodded. 'Ah. Then the wording should be: "Once the duke your father's heir discovered that you had not been provided for, he moved to correct that mistake." Yes. I think that is both truthful and acceptable. You are, after all, the previous duke's heir, in a way.'

In a way, yes. For the first time, that caused satisfaction instead of shame.

Something inside Lion eased and he sat back in his chair. He might not be able to think of Sarah as a potential wife, but he could still make sure she was cared for. As a brother should.

'Excellent. You'll act as trustee, I hope?'

Mr Lodge nodded happily. 'Naturally! And may I say, you've been most generous, Mr Trengrouse.'

He'd been as generous as he dared; as generous as he thought Sarah would accept. She'd not have to work any more, that was for certain. Melza would just have to find another governess.

For a moment, he felt a pang for the twins, who clearly loved their Miss Lamb. But they'd get over that. One did, when one's nursemaid or tutor moved on. It happened.

'Then if you will set up the trust, I'll instruct my bank to forward the funds.'

'Certainly, Mr Trengrouse.'

He'd planned to buy another ship, but

that could wait. They had enough ships for the current trade, and they could always send more via the Gunson's barques. Charles Gunson was planning on expanding their fleet, and would be glad of the business.

'Just one thing, sir,' Lodge added. 'I assume that I'm at liberty to release the funds as the young lady's dowry?'

Instinctively, he wanted to say, 'No!' Selfish. Stupid.

'Not all of it,' he said instead, remembering Petroc giving Kerenza shares in the family tin mine for her birthday because, 'A woman shouldn't be entirely dependent on her husband.'

'No, not all of it,' he went on. 'Keep some in trust, to be administered by you. So that she always has her own source of income. Perhaps half could be her dowry?'

'A substantial sum.' Mr Lodge regarded him with approval.

Lion let out a long breath. 'I don't need to say that this is in strict confidence. Hereward Langwick should know nothing about it.

Nor anyone else, including my sister's man of business.'

Mr Lodge was shocked. 'Mr Trengrouse! Discretion is our byword!'

And what his clients paid for. But having the trust administered by Hereward's own solicitor would allay any doubts Melza or Sarah might have.

He went home whistling, feeling for the first time since the ball that he'd taken a step into the future, instead of being mired in a depressing present.

His Sarah would have all the elegancies of life, and that counted for *something*.

CHAPTER 8

Sarah was having trouble parsing the letter. It couldn't say what she thought—could it? Her heart began to beat, faster and faster.

'Is everything all right, Sarah?' Demelza's voice cut through her confusion. Wordlessly, she held the letter out to her over the afternoon tea tray.

Demelza took it and read, sitting back on her chair with a hand to the small of her back. It was late October, and she was beginning to be uncomfortable.

'Good Lord! Who'd have thought it of

Hereward? I didn't think he had an ounce of family feeling!' She beamed towards Sarah. 'I'm so glad for you, my dear!'

'So…you think it's real?'

Demelza looked carefully at the letter again. 'It's certainly on the letterhead of the solicitor the Langwicks use. Papa uses them sometimes, when it's about the property Mama brought with her dowry. Mr Lodge—that's definitely the name I've heard. So, yes, my dear. I do think it's genuine.'

She was—she was *rich*!

Not Trengrouse rich, but rich enough for anyone else.

Rich enough to buy her own house. To have fires in every room, if she wanted, all the way through winter! To live in it alone.

The thought made her shiver, but she put that aside. She could—she could hire a companion as chaperone! She could *travel*.

The world opened up around her, like the unfurling of a flower.

Demelza laughed. 'I'm so happy for you—

although it breaks my heart to lose you right now.'

The twins. They were only just struggling back from losing their father. And they might be losing their home soon, too. Could she abandon them? She remembered so clearly what it was like to grieve her mother.

'I could stay…until things are settled…'

Tears rose in Demelza's eyes, and she reached across the table to press Sarah's hand. 'I shouldn't ask it of you. I really shouldn't. When you have such exciting prospects! But I'll accept gratefully, if you feel you can stay until after the baby's birth. Just until…until we are settled.' Demelza glanced down at her own letter, which lay on the side table. 'Mama is bringing my sisters for Christmas, and perhaps Ives and Katie and Petroc and Beatrice, too. She'll stay until my confinement. If you could be here until then…the new baby will take the twins' minds off things.'

One way or another. Either a baby

brother to dote over or the upheaval of moving home.

'Of course I can. I would prefer it if no one else knew about-' She gestured to the letter. 'This.'

'Quite right. It's no one's business but your own. I *do* thank you for staying, Sarah. I'm feeling quite befuddled these days.'

They smiled at one another. Somehow, over the last weeks, they had become friends. It gave Sarah a curious familial warmth; an illusion which could easily be ripped away, but lovely while she had it. She had certainly been treated better by Demelza than by any other employer, including a fire in her bedroom! She'd never had such a comfortable autumn in her life.

She read the letter again. 'Mr Lodge has requested that I go to his offices to sign some documents. In London.'

'Good. Yes. You can stay with Mama. They've removed to the London house for the Season, so that's no problem. I'll organise the carriage to take you. It's not as though I can leave the house to go travelling these days.'

Now that her pregnancy was showing, Lady Demelza had to avoid every social occasion bar Sunday church.

'Are you sure? I could go by stage...I could stay at Duke St...'

It was overwhelming. Travelling to London to see *her solicitor*!

'Nonsense, my dear. I'll send Cathy with you. She's desperate to see London, and acting as your lady's maid will be good practice for her.'

Cathy was the upstairs maid who looked after the girls and any female guests; Sarah was expected to do without a maid, which was no problem usually. She would need a maid for respectability if travelling, however.

It was two days to London. An overnight stay at an inn. A change of horses.

'Bill Coachman will organise everything for you,' Demelza said soothingly. Had she looked frightened? What nonsense! But-

'My lady, I don't have the funds...'

'Mr Lodge should have taken care of that.' Demelza took Mr Lodge's letter again, checking it carefully. 'Ah, yes. Here, where he says that he's "arranged matters" with the local bank for your transport. That means you can draw on them for your needs.'

'Go to a *bank*?'

'It's unusual, certainly, for a woman to do so.' Demelza frowned in thought. 'But you know, one needs to become accustomed to such things oneself. I'll go with you.'

Go with her to take money out of her own funds. Because she was *rich*! Because her family—her father's family, not the Trengrouses—cared enough about her to 'provide' for her. In the orphanage, they'd played this game over and over again, where a rich parent scooped them up and took them off to a life of luxury. A rich uncle would do!

THE VISIT to the bank was simple. The bank manager had had Mr Lodge's draft. He was only too happy to advance actual bank notes to her, plus some golden guineas. He would be only too happy to be her banker in future.

Sarah imagined what he'd have said to the paltry few pounds she'd managed to save over the past seven years, and smiled sourly. But her bitterness frothed away under the excitement.

'Let's buy something to break one of those guineas!' Lady Demelza said. 'You'll need some smaller coins for vails, and for buying food along the road.'

So they shopped, and bought a lovely new pair of leather gloves in York tan. She'd never owned anything half as nice. Not *new*.

Demelza patted her hand as they got back in the carriage. 'Just the beginning.' She leant back with a sigh of relief. 'I've been thinking.'

'Mm?'

'I think you should be a widow.'

Sarah laughed. 'Shouldn't I be a wife first?'

Smiling, Demelza nodded. 'Exactly. If you were to move to one of the nicer watering places. Not Bath, but perhaps that place in Yorkshire-'

'Harrogate?'

'Harrogate. Exactly. And if you were a widow… A Mrs Lamb, from some provincial town. You could establish yourself there quite creditably, and find a husband.'

An image of Endellion flashed across her mind, but she buried it firmly. 'I could never marry someone without telling them… telling them the truth.' As she had Endellion, and look at his reaction. No respectable man would marry her, unless he was a fortune hunter.

Lady Demelza brushed that off. 'Of course not. But my dear, the middling sort care about respectability, but they don't have…they don't have a *duty* to their family name. As long as there's no scandal around you, I doubt a lawyer or a doctor would care about your birth in the slightest. They might even like being related to a duke!'

A lawyer. A doctor.

She could be a doctor's wife. She could

imagine that. Helping him, perhaps, to do good. Being useful in the world. Having children.

By lying to the world about who she was.

But hadn't she been doing that all this time? As Miss Lamb, the respectable governess?

It was worth thinking about.

Once she knew where she stood.

Once she had seen *her* solicitor. In London.

CHAPTER 9

Her solicitor, Mr Lodge, smiled with avuncular kindness on her. He was hardly old enough! Sarah pushed down a spike of annoyance, aware that it was a manifestation of her nervousness.

'Just sign these papers, Miss Lamb, and your trust will begin to operate.'

The papers were thick and complex. She settled in to read them, only realising half a page down that Mr Lodge was startled.

'There's no need-' he began as he met her eyes.

'You expect me to sign a document I haven't *read*?' She raised her eyebrows at him. 'Is that what you ask of all your clients, Mr Lodge?'

Flustered, he smoothed back his already smooth hair. 'No, no, of course not. But for a young lady…there are so many terms which will be unknown to you…'

'My Latin is quite adequate, thank you.'

That stopped him. He blinked and then, astonishingly, smiled. 'I wish I could say the same for my clerks! By all means, then.'

The documents were indeed littered with Latin phrases and complex circumlocutions. The clerks, she remembered from something Mr Mandeville had once said, were paid by the word, and a kind employer gave them more words than were strictly necessary. Mr Lodge was clearly very kind.

It was all quite clear. The only exception was that the name of her benefactor was nowhere to be found. She pointed this out to

Mr Lodge, who suddenly looked uncomfortable.

'Yes, well…your—your benefactor, as you do very right to call him, prefers to keep his name out of everything.'

His name. So it wasn't the countess; she hadn't really thought it would be, but it would have been nice if, now she knew Sarah, Lady Trengrouse had been moved to greater generosity. Sarah shouldn't feel unhappy; not when *he*, the duke, had provided for her so handsomely. Also, it was entirely possible that the countess had reminded her cousin of his duties to his brother's daughter. That was a cheering thought. Even if he wanted to keep her at arm's length.

Mr Lodge fidgetted, waiting for her reply.

'Of course, the duke would not want his name associated with mine,' she said dryly.

'Dukes are careful about that kind of thing,' he agreed with equal dryness.

She realised that he was looking at her with admiration, and remembered

Demelza's words. A lawyer might not care about her illegitimacy; or might even prefer to be associated with a duke's family.

Her stomach churned; she wasn't at all sure how she felt about that.

She signed the papers with her full name: Titania Sarah Lamb. She had no birth certificate, and Titania Lamb was what was written in the ledger at the orphanage, and on her baptismal register, so that was who she was. She added the 'Sarah' in for completeness sake, so that there would never be any question of who she was and who owned this bequest.

There. It was done. Mr Lodge beamed.

'Now, I shall issue you your allowance each quarter day. I can send my clerk around to your home with it, or send you a draft upon your bank. Which would you prefer?'

The idea of having that much money in her possession made her queasy. What if she lost it? What if it were stolen?

'I'm staying with Lady Demelza until after her confinement,' she explained. 'The bank you sent the last draft to has offered to hold my account.'

'I'm sure they did. Very well, then. You have enough to go on with? Yes? You're at Mandeville House?'

'Yes, that's right. I have some commissions for Lady Demelza to perform, and then I'll be returning to Gloucestershire.' She hesitated. 'Mr Lodge…if I desired to buy a house, are you able to advance me the funds to do so?'

'If I judge it to be a sound purchase, certainly!' He hesitated in turn. 'But, my dear Miss Lamb, if I may be so bold…it might be better to withhold your funds for your dowry. A young lady of your-your looks and intelligence…with this kind of dowry, I expect you would be married within a season of you appearing at any Assembly!'

His eyes *were* admiring. Not in the salacious way she had encountered before. This was the way a man looked at a girl he considered marriageable. It was a balm to her soul. This was respectability. If part of her resented that it had been bought with money, it was at least *family* money, just as it would have been for Lady Demelza, when she met Mr Mandeville.

That was how women were valued: for looks and wealth. Now, for the first time, she had both, enough to overcome her birth for all but the highest sticklers.

'Indeed,' Mr Lodge went on, 'if I were not already married myself, I'd be on your doorstep courting you tomorrow!'

Ah.

She waited for a flicker of disappointment, but none came. Marriage to Mr Lodge —or to anyone—seemed impossible. Outside the scope of her imagination.

Imagination could be cultivated. She had time. Time and money!

From the coffee house across the street, Endellion watched Sarah leave Lodge's office, his clerk hailing a hackney for her and paying the driver up front.

She looked…satisfied.

That was good.

There was a spring in her step as she climbed into the hackney, followed by her maid. *He'd* done that! He'd made her secure and independent. It was all he could do.

He sat and stared as the hackney drove away. Inside his chest, his heart stuttered as she left. There was pain; actual, physical pain at the thought that she was leaving. His whole body shook with it.

What ridiculous weakness!

Forcing himself to his feet, he paid his shot and strode out. *Act like a man!* His father's voice echoed in his head, and for once he welcomed it.

He had an appointment with Avi to visit one of their customers, a haberdasher in the Pantheon Bazaar who was planning to set up a chain of shops in market towns across the country. They were considering investing in the scheme, which seemed like an excellent idea to them both, but they wanted some hard numbers first.

He might pick up some sweetmeats for Kerenza and Melissa while he was there. Melissa had a passion for caramels, and it would be a good excuse to take Avi to meet the family before the soirée.

His promise to Avi pushed at him. The Trengrouse soirée was always one of the first events of the Season. He'd obtained an invitation for Avi, but it would be more polite for them to visit beforehand.

SARAH AND CATH WENT SHOPPING, despite a cold wind which made Sarah thankful for the green wool pelisse Demelza had given her. Her half-boots *should* have kept her ankles warm. They didn't. Autumn was such a depressing time; summer warmth gone so quickly, days shortening, and *months* to go before they lengthened out again.

Cath walked a couple of steps behind her, which felt very odd. All through the Pantheon Bazaar, Cath trailed her as she bought the laces and ribbons and fabrics Demelza had tasked her with.

She caught a glimpse of Cath looking covetously at a length of printed muslin in pink, a colour which would suit her rose complexion and dark hair. Impulsively, Sarah bought a dress length of it out of her own money, because she *could*, and gave it to Cath to carry.

'For you,' she said. Cath stared at her, wide-eyed. What a wonderful feeling this was, to be able to give! A thing she'd never felt before. Presents weren't encouraged at the orphanage.

She bought a calico bag, too, for Cath to carry their purchases in, and some neckerchiefs for Bill Coachman and the groom who had accompanied them. And two bags of sweetmeats, for them to have on the journey —one for her and Cath, and one for the men.

Then she stopped herself. It would be *so easy* to keep spending. It was exhilarating, but dangerous. She was respectably set up, but she wasn't rich like the Trengrouses were rich. She would still have to practise economy; just at an entirely different level than previously.

At least her dresses were all good. She'd even seen a couple of women glance at her admiringly. Lady Demelza was all the crack, of course, so she was perfectly fashionable. Some of the clothes she'd been given were only a few months old.

Another source of satisfaction. No one here knew she was a bastard. All they saw was a fashionable woman of means, followed, as she should be, by her maid. It wasn't as though she were a green girl who needed a footman to keep her safe. They probably thought her a young matron, shopping for her household.

She was pierced by a longing to *be* that young matron. To have that life, that solidity, that *certainty* of belonging which a husband and family would give her.

Lady Demelza was right. She should turn herself into a widow. A widow of some years' standing, so she wouldn't need to be in mourning.

'Cath,' she said. 'Would you like to be my maid when I leave Mandeville House?'

'Oh *yes*, Miss!' Cath's eyes were wide. With the twins still so young, she had no chance of making it to lady's maid in the next decade; going with Sarah would catapult her to a better position, even if it were in a lowly household.

Understanding that, Sarah was still comforted by her ready acceptance. Cath, she knew, spoke her mind rather more than the housekeeper thought proper. If she hadn't wanted to take the job, she would have said so.

Sarah smiled at her and then looked up, caught by the sight of an Indian gentleman in perfect, dandy-like attire strolling arm-in-arm with-

Her breath caught in her chest. It *would* happen now! Just when she was feeling so good. Why *now*?

Her bright mood plummeted, and her

heart beat like a bird's. He was so handsome. So tall, graceful, strong, bringing a sense of the wild into this tame London scene.

'Oh, it's Mr Lion!' Cath said brightly.

'Let's not bother him.' Sarah forced the words out as naturally as she could. 'He's with a friend.'

Obligingly, Cath turned and they went in the other direction, back to Marlborough Street. They could find a hackney there.

She couldn't have borne it if he'd refused to acknowledge her.

The family were, of course, scrupulously courteous to Avi, but Endellion rather thought they liked him, too. It probably helped that he was already married, and therefore no romantic threat to the girls.

He handed over the sweetmeats to Melissa, who seemed touched that he had remembered her preference for caramels.

Mama was distracted by a letter from Ives.

'Ives and Katie are coming to stay for the Season! Oh, lovely, but where shall I put them? We're so full!' Her face brightened. 'Sarah Lamb won't mind removing to Mandeville House—there's always staff there, and it's just for a day or two.'

'Mama, you can't!' The force of his anger surprised him. 'She's a guest.'

'My dear, she's not *exactly* a guest. She doesn't even try to eat with us, which I think is very well done of her. She's an employee.'

'Not for long, if what Demelza tells me is true. The duke's heir has provided for her.' It wasn't a lie. Not really. 'She'll stay until the baby is born, and then make her own life.'

'Good Lord! Who on earth organised that?'

Endellion cleared his throat and looked meaningfully at her.

'Oh.' Surprisingly, Mama coloured, as though he'd accused her of something underhanded. 'I didn't think you knew about Sarah.'

'She told Melza.' Which was true, as far as it went. Melza had written him about it.

'And Melza told you. You two always were thick as thieves.'

Silence was the only prudent answer. He felt vaguely ashamed, as though tainted by his knowledge of Sarah's parentage, and of his own. That was a feeling he was accustomed to, however, so he shrugged it off.

'You can't send her away, Mama.'

'No, no, very well. Ives and Katie will just have to share a room.'

Time to take their leave. He collected Avi from his conversation with Melissa—something about the Sanskrit origins of Ancient Greek—and made his bows. He didn't kiss his mother goodbye. Most of the time, he could pretend that all was well between them; but not today.

CHAPTER 10

Returning to Gloucestershire was sobering. It was as though she were once again, and always, Miss Lamb The Governess.

That was also comforting. She didn't have to make any decisions until after the baby was born. She could just live her life and teach the twins and teach Cath, too, in her off hours, what she'd need to do as a lady's maid. That had been one of the possible jobs that girls from the orphanage were prepared for, so she knew the ins and outs of it, although the hairstyles and fashions had changed somewhat since then.

Once the baby was born, and Lady Demelza knew where she was going to live, *then* she could make plans.

A MONTH LATER, at the end of November, Demelza received a letter. She and Sarah had taken to dining together; a preview of what life would have been like for them after the girls had grown and married. Not a bad life, but Sarah was very glad she had other options now.

'Mama writes that she'll be here for Christmas.' Demelza's gaze sharpened on the page. 'And she's bringing *everyone*! Good Lord.'

'Everyone?' Her palms were suddenly clammy.

'Kerenza and Melissa and Ives and Katie. Petroc and Beatrice are bringing Bea's mother too. She wants a *family reunion*. What on Earth for? We were all together only in August!'

There was genuine puzzlement in her tone.

'The Viscount and his family too?' She wouldn't ask about Endellion. She wouldn't.

'I wouldn't be at all surprised!' Demelza looked exhausted at the thought. 'There's no problem about putting everyone up, obviously, but all of the guest rooms will have to be aired and cleaned and— Oh, Sarah, I'm sorry to ask it of you, but would you take on the planning? I just *can't* think about it all.' At seven months along, Demelza was still getting sick every morning. She'd lost weight despite all her housekeeper's cosseting, and she had half of her old energy.

'Yes, of course.'

Mandeville House was huge. Twenty-four bedrooms, not counting the servants' quarters or the rooms over the stables where the grooms slept.

It was kept well, naturally, but many of

the rooms were shut up and only opened when guests were expected.

Sarah needed to go over each one of them with the housekeeper.

There'd been an odd increase in her position in the household. Perhaps it was a consequence of her growing friendship with Demelza, but Sarah rather thought that Cath had said a word or two about her new trust fund. A penniless governess was one thing, and belonged on the rigid ladder of upper servant heirarchy. A respectable almost wealthy young woman who was staying to lend the family a hand was on quite another rung—possibly no longer on the ladder at all.

So Mrs Diccon was accommodating and polite and quite *kind*, really. She'd clearly taken it upon herself to teach Sarah how to hold household, and expanded when it became clear that Sarah was grateful for her tutelage.

They went through the house, making note of which chairs needed to be reupholstered, or swapped for ones in the attic.

Which curtains needed careful laundering. Which sheets were patched and should be turned into baby clouts. Which windows had draughts which needed caulking, which flues should be swept.

Sarah hadn't realised that Mandeville House kept its very own chimneysweep, who looked after the House, the dower house, and the three large tenant farmhouses.

'Oh yes,' Demelza said. 'We have one at home, too. Trengrouse Hall has so many chimneys, they finish and have to start all over again.'

Somehow, the idea of having one's *own chimneysweep* made her realise how rich the Trengrouses and Mandevilles were as nothing else had.

And she noted that Trengrouse Hall was somehow still 'home' to Demelza. It would be wonderful to have that; a place which was always 'home', no matter what course your life took. If the baby was a girl, no doubt Demelza and the twins would go back to Cornwall and decide on their future there.

While she would go…where?

She still had time to decide, but that time was getting shorter. And no one, yet, had told her whether Endellion was coming for Christmas.

Please God let him stay away!

CHAPTER 11

'And this one, Mrs Diccon, will be for Mr Endellion.'

Sarah was proud of herself for her lack of obvious emotion. *And* she'd given him the bedroom which best suited his status of executor of Mr Mandeville's will, rather than the poky little hole far away from everyone else she'd *wanted* to stick him in.

Unfair to him, but since she'd overcome the impulse, she didn't try to deny it existed. He'd done nothing wrong. Nothing. Just danced with her, and run with her on the beach, and made her fall in love with him.

Which was her own *blasted* fault, because she'd always known it was impossible.

'He likes this room,' Mrs Diccon said approvingly. 'Last time Mr Mandeville and his wife had it.'

Mrs Diccon clearly disapproved of Mr Mandeville and his wife; Sarah didn't know whether to agree with her or talk her out of it. Until they knew what the baby was…

She found herself hoping, for Demelza's sake, that it was a girl. That would free her to live any life she chose. Assuming, of course, that she didn't want to continue here and raise her children in their father's house.

THE GUESTS BEGAN to arrive a week before Christmas, and suddenly the quiet house was full of life and movement and noise.

First, the Cornish contingent: the earl and countess, Lady Melissa and Lady Kerenza. Lady Beatrice Marlowe and Captain Petroc Trengrouse.

Sarah braced herself to see the countess

again, but Lady Trengrouse treated her with the same absent affection she gave to her horse. Or to the girls' nanny, who had nannied her own children and had taken up residence in the nursery at Mandeville House again, released from Rosalie's care. They treated her rather like a shared favourite book, to be lent around as needed; if Nanny hadn't clearly thrived on this treatment, Sarah would have been outraged.

That evening, Ives and Katie Trengrouse appeared with Locryn's three children. Apparently Locryn and his wife Elestryn were having a Yuletide holiday. Unfortunately, Lady Kelynack arrived with them. She had taken a house nearby, 'So we can all be a family this first Christmas.' But Sir Denzell came with her, which Sarah was interested to note cheered up Demelza considerably.

The children greeted Sarah enthusiastically and Jory proceeded to describe every 'high-stepper' they had seen harnessed to every carriage they passed. In detail. The other two seemed resigned to their horse-mad brother, but the twins would have none of it.

'We're going after garlands in the woods tomorrow!' Adelia announced, and the five of them raced off together.

Endellion arrived the day after everyone else, with his Indian friend, Mr Arasan.

As luck—or the devil—would have it, Sarah was the only one available to greet them. She showed them to Endellion's door and stopped. There was no way on God's green Earth that she would go into that room with him. Best not to even open the door.

She was polite, unexceptional, while her heart pounded and she knew her face was pale. What a love-struck mooncalf she was!

Her only consolation was that he seemed as uncomfortable and as stiffly courteous as she was.

Good. She hoped he choked on it.

Anger was a far more reliable crutch than etiquette, and she embraced it with gratitude.

'If there's anything else, Mr Trengrouse, just ring and one of the other servants will attend you. Your valet?'

'I left him in London. I didn't want to wish another mouth to feed on Demelza.'

She nodded. So that coat could be shrugged in and out of instead of having to be carefully eased on by a gentleman's gentleman; the fact that it still clung to broad shoulders just showed that the shoulders were real, which she'd never doubted.

Stop looking!

'I'll send Malcolm up to unpack for you, then. This way, please, Mr Arasan. We've put you in the tower room.' She dropped a brief curtsey and left. There. Perfectly appropriate.

To stop the tears, she clenched her hands tightly so that her fingernails cut into her palm. She might not be a lady, but she could act like one.

'What a lovely house, Miss Lamb,' Mr Arasan said. Was he being kind, making conversation?

'Yes. Parts of it are very old, such as the tower where your room is. Through here.' She opened the big old Gothic door and led him to one of her favourite rooms, a round room with small windows, where the girls played Rapunzel. 'Just ring if you need anything.'

She stood back to let him go through the door, and turned to leave, but he put out a hand. Was this another privileged man who thought a governess was fair game? Her stomach twisted.

'Miss Lamb, I wonder if I might seek your advice? My wife wants me to find an English governess to bring home with me, to prepare my girls for their come-out. Perhaps you know of someone?'

Oh, how she'd love to say, 'Yes! Take me!' The idea of India was enchanting. Part of her yearned to set sail and follow the rising sun, to explore places she'd only read about. But that would tie her just as closely to Endellion as working for Demelza did.

'I'll give it some thought, Mr Arasan.'

'I'd be most obliged, Miss Lamb.' He bowed. A proper bow, too, not just a bob of the head. It comforted her in some obscure way she didn't want to examine.

Her curtsey this time was properly respectful.

AS SHE WALKED AWAY, back straight, next to Avi, Lion had to face it. The pounding of his heart made him confront the truth.

He loved her still.

Surely he wasn't so debased? *Surely* he couldn't still desire her, knowing she was his sister? It was impossible. Disgusting.

Deep in his soul, a part of him refused to accept that. Refused to admit it. She was *his*, goddammit!

It was a soul-deep knowing, and no rational thought seemed to work against it. He'd tried. God knows he'd tried.

There was only one cure. He'd have to hear confirmation from his mother's own lips. If *she* confirmed that Sarah was his sister, he'd leave. Go to the ends of the earth to get some distance and some perspective.

He needed to hear Mama say it. Now.

If she confirmed it…

That would be the end.

He found his mother in the morning room, just sitting, a letter before her but no quill in her hand. Staring off into space. Worrying about some member of the family. Ives, perhaps, or Melissa? She wanted to find a husband for Melissa, Petroc had written him, which wasn't a task for the faint-hearted.

At least she was alone.

On the other side of the room was a door to the library, so he went over and opened it to check. No one there. They could talk in peace.

Mama regarded him with astonishment.

'What on Earth are you doing, Endellion?' She only ever called him that when she was cross with him. It wasn't a good start.

He stood before her as he had so many times as a child and young man, called to account for bad behaviour. Looking back, he didn't think he'd been any worse than the other boys, but somehow he was the one who always got into trouble. Too bloody conspicuous, that was his problem; his brothers merged into one dark-headed troop, while he stood out. Always. Punished more severely than them by his father, too.

'I need to speak with you, Mama.'

'Apparently so. Sit down, for Heaven's sake!'

He couldn't sit. He took two steps across the small room and turned, paced back, stopped. Under his ribs, his heart beat so hard he thought it might leave a bruise.

'I need the truth about my parentage.'

Confusion crossed her face. 'I beg your pardon? What are you talking about?'

Say it. Just *say it*.

'I need to know who my father is.'

'Who your *father* is?' She rose, a hand to her heart. Hah. She'd thought him ignorant. Urgency took him by the throat. He had no hope, but he had to *know*, for certain. before he could banish this feeling for Sarah.

'I *need* to know, Mama. Is Sarah Lamb my sister?'

She had gone deathly white. Then two circles of red flamed on her cheeks.

'How *dare* you? How dare you even *suggest..?*' She was choked with anger. But that didn't mean she wasn't guilty. Of course she'd be angry.

'I'd like to know the truth too.' The voice came from behind them. They spun around as one. Papa, in the doorway to the library. '*Is the boy her brother?*'

Mama reached out to the desk to support herself.

'Jory-' Taking a deep breath in, she let it out slowly, as if trying to control herself, but then snapped. 'You're both insulting. Despicable. *Horrible!*'

'Even so, I need to know, Mama.'

Her mouth was set in a tight line, her grey eyes—the Beaufort eyes which he and Sarah shared—bleak.

'Your father was Jory Trengrouse.' Her gaze flicked to his father. 'I have *never* betrayed my wedding vows, and I never would. James Beaufort was my cousin, and nothing more.'

'Nothing?' His father's voice was full of disbelief.

She whirled on him, and Lion realised he'd never seen her truly angry before. 'Did I love him? Oh yes, I did. I adored him. If he hadn't been my first cousin, I would have married him. I would have married him anyway, if both our sets of parents hadn't objected. I would have waited until our majority, applied for the dispensation for cousins to marry, and bedamned to all of them! But James wasn't prepared to defy both man *and* God to be with me.' She faltered, her hand going again to just under her heart. 'So I married you, and I have been faithful to you, as I will be unto death. Not that *you* deserve it!'

There were tears in her eyes. She stared at Papa and he stared back, ashen. The feeling of unsaid years of suspicion was in the air.

'And,' she went on, 'if your attitude to me all these years was because you thought Endellion was James', then you're not only insulting, you're a damned fool!' She rounded on Endellion. 'Sarah Lamb is a bastard. The daughter of an opera singer, and not fit to marry into this family, but she's not a light-skirt, and I won't have you offer her a carte blanche!'

She grabbed a handkerchief from the desk and walked out, leaving both of them without words.

Endellion was frozen. He'd had no idea his parents' marriage was so uncertain. They put on such a good show of unanimity.

But under that worry was…peace, at long last. And guilt.

All these years, he had misjudged her. Just as his father had. Lion had no doubt that Mama had spoken the truth. Judging by the pale, shaking hand Papa put to his mouth, neither did he. Good. Vindication was sweet.

Would he have ever have doubted her if his father had treated him as he did his brothers?

'I always knew you didn't love me as you did the others,' he said. 'I thought it was *my* fault, until I received that inheritance, and read the duke's will on my majority. Then I understood.' He hadn't forgiven it, though. The pain of being cut out of his father's heart couldn't yield to an adult understanding of the reason.

Jory Trengrouse was diminished, stooping like an old man.

'I tried not to let it show.'

'Did you? It didn't work.'

He was so much taller than his father. His actual father. His father by blood. Cousin James had merely been his godfather, and the inheritance simply a good deed. His imaginings of what life would have been like with his 'real' father were a boy's fantasies. *This* was his father, and would be forever. The man who had taken out his own pain on an innocent boy.

'Perhap we can…' his father began. Lion cut him off.

'Oh, I think it's too late for that, don't you? We don't have much to do with each other any more. No need for some Drury Lane melodrama which ends in reconciliation. We'll just go on as we have been.'

Papa gave a short, sharp nod.

Lion returned it, and left, not even realising he was fighting tears until one dropped on his jacket.

Nonsense. There was no need to be maudlin. His mother wasn't a drab and, more importantly, Sarah Lamb was *not* his sister.

There was no barrier to their marriage.

The heaviness lifted from him, as though he were filled with light. His whole body seemed to expand with happiness.

Time to propose properly.

CHAPTER 12

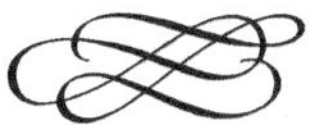

He couldn't just turn up her bedroom door out of the blue. Not without causing a scandal. Yet that was the only place he could be sure of finding her alone.

They'd have to meet somewhere.

He had appointments as John's executor all afternoon: the steward, tenants with complaints about the steward, the estate solicitor.

When they got back to his bedroom, he had just enough time before dinner to write her a note, but he didn't know what to say.

He sat there for fifteen minutes, trying to find the right words. Dashed hard to invite a girl to an assignation without it seeming shady.

His valet brought in his evening clothes. Another bloody family dinner. With guests—Katie's mother Lady Kelynack and Denzell her brother as well.

No idea what to say. Perhaps it would be better to just ask her for a meeting?

A girl was allowed to be alone with a man when it was a case of a marriage proposal.

And then what? What if she said yes, what would they do?

There was no hope that his family would endorse the marriage, so it would have to be special license. Then where would they go? London Society would turn a cold shoulder once they found out the truth—and they *would* find out, they always did. There'd be someone who remembered Sarah's father and mother. There'd be someone from the orphanage who'd sell her out for a few shillings.

The possibilities tumbled over and through his mind, and all he was sure of was that he loved her, and he had to protect her from harm. How, he didn't know.

He hadn't thought it through, and he must.

The outcome, though… Sarah's eyes on the night of ball…he hadn't imagined the light in them. The desire. If he could just be *with* her again, he knew it would all turn out as it should.

They would work it out together.

How odd it was to see the family arrayed together like this, and to be invited to be a part of it. Demelza had roundly rejected Sarah's suggestion that she eat in her room, as a governess should.

'I *need* you there! Honestly, the whole thing is insane! I have no idea why Mama's insisted on us all being together this year! And she wants the children at the dinner too! Please come and keep an eye on them.'

Ah. Sarah tried not to be hurt that she *was*, in fact, there as a governess and not as a family friend. It did make the dinner itself easier, as she and the children were at the far end of the table. Since there was no host, the master's seat at the table was vacant. Tradition should have had the earl, as the highest ranking man present, take that spot, but instead Demelza put the younger Jory there, and the other children around him. Sarah sat between Rosalie and Adelia, and counted herself lucky that she didn't have to make conversation with the adults.

After dinner, she was shepherding the children up to prepare for bed, when Demelza caught at her sleeve.

'Leave them to Nanny. She'll love having all of them. Come back and play for us?'

Sarah nodded reluctantly. She was happy to play at any time, but there had been an odd atmosphere at dinner. The earl and countess had barely glanced at one another, and Endellion had been quiet too, with an air of repressed tension. Demelza had virtually ignored Sir Denzell, and Katie was pale, as though ill. Lady Kelynack, fortunately, had talked non-stop, so the others could pretend to simply listen to her, although eyes were glazing over all around the table.

No wonder Demelza wanted her to play; it was the only way to get Lady Kelynack to be quiet. Sarah smiled as she handed the children over to a delighted Nanny. She'd pick something long. A sonata, perhaps.

When she approached the pianoforte in the drawing room, everyone sat up with an air of relief.

'Oh, lovely!' Demelza cut across Lady Kelynack's diatribe about the deplorable state of the roads in Gloucestershire. 'Thank you, Sarah, some music would be lovely.'

Endellion sprang to her side. 'I'll turn the pages.'

She laughed, trying hard to look as though she were unaffected by his nearness. By the scent of his cologne. The warmth of his body. 'I don't have any pages. I'll play from memory.' He blinked, confused, and then lowered his head and spoke softly.

'Meet me in the library before you go up. *Please.*'

After that, she *did* need music, because every note went out of her heard. Instead of the sonata, she played a series of folk songs, heart pounding, mind whirling.

Should she go?

Could she bear to *not* go? The curiosity would kill her.

It occurred to her that, just possibly, he might know about her inheritance, and saw it as a way to have...to have access to her outside marriage. If she were independent, in a house of her own... Would he offer her a carte blanche?

What would she say if he did?

LION SLID OUT EARLY. 'LONG DAY,' he muttered, and Demelza nodded at him, one ear on Lady Kelynack's latest anecdote, one ear on Sarah's music. How rude that woman was, talking through her performance! She wouldn't have done so if Kerenza had been playing, but the governess was a person of no account to someone like her.

He waited in the library. At least there was a fire, which gave him something to do: feed it a log, rattle it with a poker, get ash on his breeches, brush the breeches off. Listen to the perfect melodies trailing through the air, and try to catch his breath.

He'd done many things his family disapproved of, but none would match this.

The music stopped, and his heart stuttered. Hastily, he checked his hair in the mirror over the fireplace, and smoothed it back.

Sarah came in quietly. She *came*. By the sound of things, the others were still in the drawingroom, talking. The noise was cut off as the door closed.

They were alone.

He waited, not wanting to spook her with a sudden movement. It felt like that; as though she were a timid bird, and he had to coax her nearer.

She did move closer, but stopped at the edge of the rug, and put her hand on the back of one of the armchairs.

'Well, Mr Trengrouse?'

Chilly. No wonder, the way he'd treated her at the ball. And of course she didn't know about the money.

He had no idea what to say. His throat closed up, his mouth dry. Sweaty palms, heart galloping—he was like a moonstruck lad. He coughed and forced out, 'Marry me.'

She blinked.

'I beg your pardon?'

'Marry me.' It was easier to say the second time. 'I mean, Miss Lamb, would you do me the very great honour of becoming my wife?'

'Are you foxed?' Her face was stern, and somehow *hurt*. 'Or is this a joke?'

That jolted him.

'Of course it's not a joke! I want to marry you, goddammit!'

'Don't be ridiculous. You know it's impossible.' She looked suddenly green, as though she were going to be sick. He made an instinctive move towards her, and she jerked away, so he froze.

'Please, Sarah. Listen to me.'

Listen to him? Listen to him destroy his life? And hers? Even solitary respectability would be better than the scandal-broth he'd plunge them both into.

Wouldn't it?

'I-I thought you'd offer me a carte blanche.' Her lips felt numb. Her hands were shaking.

'I'd *never*!' He sounded quite offended, which made her laugh. 'You don't understand,' he added.

'It seems quite clear. You want to ruin your life.' Unsteady, she moved to sit on the arm of the chair. Images of married life—marriage to *Endellion*—began to dance through her head. Together. Breakfast, church on Sunday…the marriage bed. Suddenly hot, she dragged a hand across her face.

'No. No, you don't understand, and how could you?' He sat in the other armchair and looked up at her, his face determined. 'I've never told anyone else this…the reason I was so, so distant to you at the ball is that, at the time, I believed your father, the duke, was my father too.'

The idea hit her with a thump of revulsion. It must have showed on her face, because he hurried on. 'It's not true. I found out only today, it's not true. My mother…she was faithful. We're not brother and sister. But at the time-'

'Why on *Earth* would you think otherwise?' He was taller and blonder than the others, but surely that wouldn't be enough to put that idea into someone's head?

'My father…treated me differently. When your father died, I inherited an estate from him. Henwood Hall, in Little Foxbury. And his will…the will said it was due to "the paternal feeling I have towards him". He was my godfather, you see, but taken with all the rest...I assumed.'

What a bumble-bath! Of course, believing that, when she'd told him the duke was her father, he'd reacted as he did. Something eased inside her; that had hurt a great deal but was robbed of its sting.

Then something else penetrated. Henwood Hall. The documents the solicitor had given her had mentioned that her income was derived from the rents on Henwood Hall.

'*You*! *You're* the one who organised my—what they said was my inheritance!'

He jumped to his feet, dismayed.

'Henwood Hall!' She had no idea how she felt.

'I thought you were my sister! Of course I provided for you!'

'Without telling me.'

That was the insult. That was what she couldn't look past. He had, like everyone else she'd known, disposed of her life as though he had the right to make her decisions. How *dare* he!

Of course he'd done it without telling her.

'You wouldn't have taken it otherwise,' he pleaded.

'If you'd told me you were my brother, I would have.'

Oh. That had never crossed his mind. He'd arbitrarily organised her life for her as though he had the right, without giving her any reason or involving her in any way. Melissa had lectured him on Wollstonecraft's The Rights of Women often enough that he could see where he'd erred.

'I'm sorry. I should have explained everything, and asked what you wanted me to do.'

That took the wind out of her sails. Was it bad for him to be glad of that? He didn't want this to end in recriminations.

'I love you,' he said gently. Cautiously, he went to stand by her side. She looked up at him with troubled eyes. 'Sweetheart, I've loved you since the first moment I saw you, at James' funeral. You tipped me a settler right then and there, and I've never recovered. Please say that you'll marry me.'

Tears rose in her eyes, and she dashed them away. He took that hand and held it tight. It shook in his grasp.

'Could you perhaps come to love me too?'

She laughed brokenly. Pulling her hand away, she stood up and looked him square in the eyes. 'I can't marry you.'

Without another word, she walked out, and he was left standing there, empty-handed, cold as ice despite the roaring fire, his breath caught in his chest, and not a single clue about what to do next.

CHAPTER 13

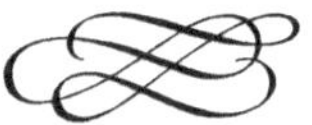

She needed to be ruthless again.

Ruthlessly, she forced herself to not think about marriage.

Think about the money. She couldn't take it now. She *would* have taken it, gladly, if it had come from a brother. But he *wasn't* her brother, so that didn't apply.

She needed help. Demelza had gone up to bed, but only a few minutes ago. She wouldn't be asleep yet.

· · ·

LADY DEMELZA REGARDED her with shocked eyes.

'He wants to-'

'Yes, my lady. He says he wants to marry me. Obviously, that is *quite* ineligible. And worse—*he* was the source of my so-called "inheritance". Of course I can't take any of it, now I know.'

Sarah could barely talk around the stone lodged in her throat. The vision of marrying Lion was drifting away from her with every word. Which was right and good. If she loved him, she had no business ruining him, and marriage to her *would* ruin him. It almost broke her that the vision of independent spinsterhood was shattered at the same time.

Demelza blinked.

'Oh, that's just like Lion. I could slap him! If that ever got out, your reputation would be *gone!*'

She hadn't even thought about that. Bile climbed the back of her throat. She swallowed it down.

Demelza paced back and forth with some of her old energy.

'You're quite right about the marriage. It would be disastrous. There'd be no keeping your parentage secret. The scandal would engulf the whole family. Including the twins.' She put a hand on her abdomen. 'There's enough talk now, about this baby and what might happen.'

'Which is why I need your help. I can't stay, but I do need a way to hide.'

Demelza's gaze sharpened. 'Yes. As long as he can find you, he won't give up. Lion never gives up on anything once he's decided on it. Look at how he went to India. It seemed pure foolishness, but it has allowed him to amass quite a large fortune.'

'I'm not interested in a large fortune.'

That Trengrouse chin came up. 'May I ask why not, Sarah? Forgive me, but if I were in your shoes, the opportunity to make a good marriage—an *excellent* marriage— would be very attractive. Why aren't you grasping it with both hands?'

What could she say which wouldn't sound appallingly missish? She felt the blush rise in her cheeks, and Demelza sighed.

'You're in love with him. Bother. He *is* handsome, I suppose.'

'Very,' she said dryly. 'He's also very kind.'

'Oh yes. Yes, he is. As kind as Felix, which is saying something. Especially to those who are on the margins of things. He was quite the hero of the boys who were bullied at Harrow, apparently.'

Harrow? Jory had told her, self-importantly, that *all* the Trengrouse boys went to Eton. Excluded, even in his own family. No wonder he'd believed himself misbegotten. Compassion and love and the need to *help* him swamped her.

India.

He'd gone to India.

Mr Arasan wanted a governess for his children. In India. Which was a very long way away.

Could she possibly just...go? Leave everything she'd ever known? Not just her life here, but her country, her culture? The thought was a mix of thrilling and terrifying.

Better that than ruining Endellion. She was cross with him about the 'inheritance', but it also gave her a deep warmth. He had cared enough to go through that elaborate charade, so that her life would no longer be precarious. That was worth a great deal, even if she couldn't take the money. She couldn't smash his life to pieces in return.

And there was the rest of the family, who would also be hurt. Bright, laughing Kerenza, yet to find a spouse. Sweet, odd Melissa: would her fiancé drop her if she was embroiled in a scandal? Men had done so before.

Even the countess…perhaps she wasn't the kindest of women, but she had cared for Sarah, in her own way. Wrecking her family would be a poor repayment for all those extra lessons and clothes, for her positions in good families. For that lamb which had comforted her through the darkest days of her grief.

She couldn't do it, no matter how much she yearned for Endellion.

'India,' she said. 'Mr Arasan is looking for a governess for his children.'

'Perfect!' Demelza was suddenly full of energy. 'You can go with him when he leaves, and in the meantime, keep to the schoolroom. I'll get my maid to pack all your things.'

Perhaps she looked alarmed, because Demelza stopped pacing and patted her arm. 'You won't suffer for your care of my little brother, Sarah. I promise you. You can come back to London or to here later.'

After Endellion had come to his senses and married someone else, was the unspoken part of that. The thought shouldn't hurt her so much; surely it was what she wanted. For him to be happy, even if that happiness was with someone else.

No. She was not at all generous where Endellion was concerned. She would protect him from himself, but she just *couldn't* wish him happy with someone else. The thought twisted her heart and stole all the breath from her lungs. It was much worse than having all that money snatched away from her, though that was a hard blow.

Years of not showing emotion lest she be punished for it came in remarkably handy when your heart was breaking.

'I'll talk to him in the morning on your behalf,' Demelza said.

Talk to Endellion?

'I'll make sure you're properly chaperoned on the voyage out.'

No, not Endellion. Mr Arasan. Of course.

Panic rose in her, but she pushed it down. Ruthlessly.

She had a plan of escape. That was the main thing.

CHAPTER 14

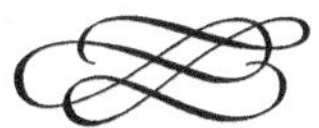

Mr Arasan, astonishingly, was less pleased than cautious.

'Have you-er-does Endellion know this plan?' he asked carefully.

Demelza and Sarah both stared him down.

'I can't see why this could possibly concern my brother,' Demelza said, frostily aristocratic.

'It does *not* concern him,' Sarah said firmly. 'It's none of his business, no matter what he might have told you.'

'What he *told* me-' Mr Arasan rubbed the

back of his head as though playing for time. '-was that he was in love with you.'

That thudded into Sarah like a kick, but she rallied.

'I'm not responsible for the ill-thought-out affections of any gentleman.'

His eyes widened. Hah! Take that! The churning in her stomach made a mockery of her bravado, but this was for *Lion*.

'If you don't wish to engage my services, Mr Arasan, I shall look elsewhere.'

Hastily, he put out a hand. 'No, no, I'd be very pleased…my wife will be over the moon, and I know the girls will like you. The only thing is…after I leave here, I go straight to the ship. We sail on Thursday. To make the ship, I'll need to leave on Tuesday.'

Tuesday. Then Thursday. Demelza didn't need her any more, not with her sisters here. Thursday, to walk up a gangplank and into a new life.

'In winter?' Demelza asked in horror.

'Winter here, but summer going around the Cape of Good Hope, which I assure you I prefer. And from there to Colombo, then Puducherry, and then home. No more than three or four months.'

The strange names were like a beacon. Her mind was a mixture of dread and longing and a sliver of hope and excitement. If she had to leave Demelza, if she had to give up her new-found security, at least she would have an adventure.

'I'll be ready to leave with you on Tuesday. On the condition that you say nothing to Mr Trengrouse—nothing *at all* about my employment with you.' Her voice was steady —nothing short of a miracle.

A quick frown went across his face, but it smoothed away when Demelza said, 'For his own sake, Mr Arasan. Miss Lamb and I are agreed that such a marriage would be unsuitable for all concerned.'

Mr Arasan smiled, a wry, twisted smile. 'I see. Very well, then. I shall say nothing.'

'Now, how will she be chaperoned on the journey? And what is your idea of a proper rate of pay for an exceptional English governess?' Demelza was all business, which was just as well. Sarah couldn't have negotiated a single thing.

She sat bonelessly in the library chair and stared out the window at the snow coming down. The children would want to go out to collect greenery and decorate the house soon. She could do that.

Performing all her duties until Tuesday would be the easy part.

Sarah was avoiding him. She had kept to the schoolroom, or surrounded herself with children, every waking moment of the day. She didn't have lunch or dinner with the family, and she didn't come in to play the pianoforte after dinner.

Christmas Day itself he spent in a vain effort to get her alone, and ended with Demelza confronting him in his own bedroom at the end of the night.

'Leave her alone, Lion,' she ordered. 'For pity's sake. She's not going to change her mind, so stop harrying her.'

'I haven't been!'

'You've been following her and the children around. Even Lady *Kelynack* noticed! I excused it away by you being a good uncle, but that excuse won't stand. Leave her be. This is harder on her than on you.'

He gave a bark of disbelief, and she waved a finger at him.

'You've lost your love. All right. That's sad. But *she's* lost her security. She won't take your money, and that means she's stuck in her job as a governess.'

Endellion stood still. No. Surely she'd see that she *deserved* that money.

'But-'

'No. I don't know what possessed you to set it up in the first place, if you wanted to marry her anyway, but she won't take it. She *can't*. It would be wholly reprehensible of her to do so, *especially* now she's refused you.'

She walked out as fast as her now-large body would allow, leaving him sunk in guilt.

If he hadn't proposed, Sarah would, at least, be safe. Cared for, for life.

He was a fool. It wasn't as though she loved him. If she had, she would have accepted him, and everything would be all right.

That wasn't true. There'd be the devil to pay and no pitch hot when the rest of the family found out he was marrying a bastard —and a *family* bastard at that! Bedamned to the lot of them. He'd always been on the outer. If he had Sarah, he wouldn't need any of them.

Couldn't make life harder for her now, though. He'd stay away. But when he got back to London, he was going to pin Hereward down and *make* him support her! She couldn't say no to her actual uncle providing for her.

The plan comforted him, but it was still a long dreary time before he fell asleep.

. . .

SAYING goodbye to the twins was hard. She'd come to love them dearly.

'I'll send you a present from India,' she said at last, after they'd clung to her and cried. 'But the ships are slow, so it will take a long time. It will be midsummer or even later before it arrives.'

That diverted them: Adelia wanted to know what the present would be, and Grace was astonished at the time it would take.

So she left them with Nanny and the atlas, said goodbye to Demelza and the new baby, and slipped out of the house to the stables, where her luggage was already strapped onto the coach Mr Arasan had hired. She was to be in it, hiding, before they brought it round for him at the front door.

It was a freezing day, grey and lowering, so no one should come out to see him go.

As the carriage rounded the house, she looked, despite herself, for Endellion, but only Mr Arasan came out of the house.

Was it possible to live without a heart? Her chest felt hollowed out, like a melon with its sweet centre eaten away. She would not cry. Not in front of her new employer.

That thought steadied her and she greeted him with tolerable composure.

'Let's be off then.' He smiled at her kindly, and she managed to smile back. He shivered with cold. 'I can't wait to be back home, where it's always warm!'

Well. That was a benefit she hadn't considered. It cheered her a little. Sitting back, she engaged Mr Arasan in conversation about his daughters. She should learn as much about them as she could before she arrived.

Because she had to be the very best English governess India had ever seen, so that when they left for London in a couple of years, she would be besieged by further offers of employment.

That was best. For everyone.

The children descended the staircase in a whoop and headed towards the kitchen.

Lion put out a hand to stop the twins as they went past.

'Where is Miss Lamb, girls?' Endellion asked. He *wasn't* harrying her, but it seemed strange that he hadn't at least seen her with the children for a couple of days.

'She's in *India*!' Adelia said.

'No, silly, it takes *months* to get to India, she told us!' Grace said, pleased to be able to correct Adelia, just this once. 'She's only on the ship to India now.'

Wildly, he looked for Demelza, but of course she was in her bedroom. He couldn't burst in. He couldn't ask Mama. Who else?

The maids would know.

He cornered one, a downcast looking-girl putting sheets away in a linen closet.

'Do you know when Miss Lamb left?'

'Tuesday!' And she burst into tears. 'Without *me!* She said she wanted to take me but Mr Arasan said best for her to have an Indian maid.' She cheered up a little. 'But missus says I can train as a lady's maid with Tancred, and she'll give me a good character.'

'Oh. Well. Fine.'

Hastily, he gave her a handkerchief and got away from there.

Avi. That *traitor*. He'd lured her away for his blasted children. How *could* he! How could she?

Remembering the look in her eyes when she'd said, 'I can't marry you,' he knew why. She'd run away from him, as though he were a poison.

He was sick to his stomach with the pain of that; and the guilt. If only he'd left well enough alone! It was enough to make a man go to the devil.

But before that, he'd damn well *force* the bloody Duke of Langwick do his duty by Sarah!

CHAPTER 15

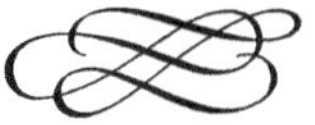

TANJORE, INDIA: FIVE MONTHS
LATER

Sarah smiled at Uma and finished playing the waltz as the girl ended her pretend dance and sank into a curtsey. The pianoforte went out of tune so quickly in this climate; she would have to organise the tuner to come next week.

'Well done, Uma. But the depth of the curtsey depends on who you've danced with. That curtsey was deep enough for a duke!'

Uma smiled serenely, and her sister Tamarai laughed and twirled in place. Mr Arasan had told her they'd been named after goddesses, but he'd got it backwards: Tamarai, named for the calm lotus of goddess Laksmi, was full of energy and always moving, whereas Uma, named for the goddess of energy, Parvati, was always calm.

They were delightful girls, hard working and very kind to her. And so pretty! Their dark eyes were alight with intelligence, their straight black hair glowed, and their faces… well, if they didn't make a stir in London with those faces and those dowries, not to mention being actual princesses in this country, she'd be very surprised.

Not that she'd see it. She'd be with some other family. Looking out the window at Tanjore's huge, sprawling temple, she hoped that wherever her next post was, she could still see this extraordinary architectural creation. She never tired of gazing at its intricate carvings.

Well, when she moved on, at least she'd

be here, in this beautiful, verdant, *warm* place. The thought of going back made her shiver.

'Now,' she said, 'let's practise our English writing.'

One of the housemen came to the door and knocked, staying well back. 'Miss Lamb? Visitor.'

How odd. She'd met a few people here, but no one who had the social entrée which would allow them to just visit. These things were far more organised than in London.

She set the girls a writing task and followed the houseman to one of the many salons. When she'd agreed to come to India, she'd never dreamed she'd be living in a palace. One of the smaller palaces, granted, but still! A marvel of workmanship, carved stone, paint and fabric, all set to catch the breezes.

How lovely it was to be always warm!

Mr Arasan's aunt, the princess known as Rani Parivu, was waiting at the door of the salon, to preserve her reputation—and, by extension, the family's. Although the princess had always been very kind to her.

The door was opened by the houseman, and Sarah paused. No one there. Was this a trick? Then someone moved from behind an embroidered panel, and her heart stopped.

Lion.

Blood surged to her face, her fingertips, her toes. It felt as though she were going to explode. Then it all rushed away, and she swayed, dizzy.

He sprang forwards, and held her up by her elbows.

'My dear, I've startled you. I'm sorry.'

Rani Parivu moved closer and glared until Lion released her. She and the princess sank into European-style chairs, instead of the traditional cushions on the floor.

'Rani Parivu, this is-'

'I know,' she said, not looking impressed. Of course. Endellion was Mr Arasan's business partner. Of course she would know him.

'How are you, Rani Amma?' Endellion

asked, but Rani Parivu just sniffed in disdain, but there was a small smile at the corner of her mouth. Rani Amma meant queen mother —a term of respect. He had lived here. He knew the etiquette, the people. It cast a new light on him. She still didn't understand—

'What-what are you doing here?'

'I've come to bring you news.'

'News?' What news could he have brought which wouldn't better be sent in a letter?

'News from your uncle. Hereward, Duke of Langwick.' Anxiously, he looked for permission to sit from the princess. At her nod, he sat in a chair next to her, leaning forward anxiously as though to catch her if she fell. She was more settled now, although her pulse beat in her veins like a captive bird's wings.

Lion handed her a letter. She received it dumbly. What could this *be*? It seemed beyond her to open it. All she could do was stare at him. He was thinner. He looked worn, as though by trouble, and older. Still so handsome; even more so, she thought, with this new air of maturity.

'Aren't you going to look at it?'

She took a breath and gazed at it. She couldn't bear it if it were one more rejection. But would he have brought her such a thing? Surely not. 'Tell me. You tell me.'

'He's ceded you a small property.'

'Not Henwood!'

A smile—such a kind smile–spread across his face. 'No, Henwood is mine. This is on the other side of the county. Derbyshire, you know. It's only a small place, but there's enough to it that you'll never need to worry. Or work.'

This up and down of her fortunes was ridiculous! Like some tawdry melodrama.

'But *why*?'

His mouth firmed and she was immediately on fire; that mouth had kissed her, once. She knew something else.

'You. You did it.'

'I pointed out to him that he had a duty to his dependants, yes. He's not such a bad fellow, Hereward. More careless than anything else. Once he'd heard and understood your position, he was happy to do it.'

'Why did you come? This could have been mailed, or sent with your business courier.' She made her voice gentle, and tried not to be accusing; he still flinched.

'Demelza…' He got up, pacing around the room. He stopped by the arched window, where the sun came through and lit his hair into a crown of gold. 'I was a sorry sight, after you left. Went to the devil a bit. Drank too much, that kind of thing. When Melza came to London to finally collect John's things from the townhouse, she…she was worried about me.' He ran a hand through his hair and stared at his boots. 'She told me you came here because you *loved* me, not because you didn't.'

His gaze came up and caught hers, naked with need and longing. Her own need surged in response, and she was on her feet without meaning to move. Lion came forward, step by step, until he stood before her, just out of reach.

'Do you love me, Sarah?'

'This marriage is impossible. You *know* it is!'

'Yes.' He agreed. Her whole body tensed. 'A normal marriage, in England, in London, would be impossible without damaging the whole family.'

There was a kind of relief in hearing him admit it, even while it hurt.

'So, what does it matter if I love you?'

'It matters.' She'd never heard him speak in that tone. Such honest need. The man had come half-way around the planet to ask that question. She couldn't lie or pretend.

'Yes, then. I love you.' A deep breath; she let it out. Part of her felt lighter. Saying it had freed her from some chain she hadn't realised was there. She was her mother's daughter after all. 'Yes and yes and yes, and if you want me to be your mistress, I will!'

He caught her in his arms and kissed her.

.　.　.

She loved him!

Her mouth was soft and welcoming, her arms went around him, his head was swimming with a delirium of desire and love and joy.

Rani Amma was suddenly there, scolding rapidly in Tamil.

'It's all right,' he said to her. 'We're going to be married.'

'No kissing before marriage!' she said sternly, in English. 'No kissing! This is the rule!'

Sarah laughed giddily, and moved away far enough to satisfy her.

'It's all right, your highness. It's over now.' She turned to Lion. 'You just said we *weren't* getting married!'

'Not in England, no.'

This was it. The only hope he had.

'I don't-'

'What I'm *hoping* is that you like India enough to stay here. With me.' Her face showed astonishment and something like alarm. He hurried on. 'I've spoken to Avi.

He'll go to London and run the show from there. Just a couple of years earlier than he thought. He was waiting for his younger brother to be old enough to take over here. Much better for me to do that and train the brother up to be a partner. So we could marry here. Live *here*.'

'But your family! The scandal!' she protested. He loved her for her care of them, but right now he wished them all to the devil. That wasn't an argument he could use; he'd had three and a half months on the ship to think of others.

'No one in England really cares what happens in India. I promise you. All they'll know is that I married some English girl. And even if people *do* find out, it's *India*. The other side of the world. It won't affect the family in anything like the same way. As long as we stay away long enough, it will just be put down to the same eccentricity which brought me to India in the first place.'

It was true. When he'd returned from India the first time, he'd been considered odd for going, but he'd been asked barely a handful of questions, and most of those were about tiger shooting, a thing he'd never done. The English just weren't that *interested*.

'You..you'd leave your home? Your family? Your country?'

He smiled helplessly. He probably looked like a sap; he didn't care. 'Beloved, *you* are my home. Wherever you are, I'll be happy.'

Tears rose in her eyes. Was he asking too much? He hurried into speech.

'If you don't want to marry me, you can still go back to England and live in your house. It's your choice.'

HER CHOICE. For the first time. The first time *ever*. And Endellion had given it to her.

'And if I chose that, you'd leave me alone? Let me live my life without you?' His tender smile became a little smug.

'Well, I would if you *wanted* me to. You did just admit you loved me, though, so it would be quite hard to convince me. But if you're prepared to stay here, we can be married straight away.'

'No no,' Rani Parivu said. 'It takes a month at least to prepare for a wedding.' She was smiling approvingly at him, though, and at Sarah. Why did that make her feel better about accepting him? Yet it did.

She smiled up at him, a little tearily.

'I…'

'Say it, beloved.'

'I do love you, Endellion Trengrouse. I will marry you.'

He let out such a whoop of joy that the girls *and* their brothers came running, followed by half the household, including Mr Arasan. Lion grabbed her and spun her around, both of them laughing, with Rani Parivu protesting vigorously.

'Lion, please!' Sarah said breathlessly. 'It's not *done*!'

'A little decorum in front of my daughters, please, Trengrouse.' That was Mr Arasan, his eyes dancing but his tone grave. He meant it.

'That's right, Lion. I'm their *chaperone*.'

She pushed him away, but smiled such a smile she felt her face would never go back to its old expression.

'Well, girls,' she said to Uma and Tamarai. 'It appears that I'm staying, and you are both going to London much sooner than expected.'

They squealed with joy and bombarded their father with questions, the boys joining in.

Endellion looked at her with tenderness.

'I swear, my dearest, you shall never have cause to regret your choice.'

His long fingers came up to touch her cheek, and she turned her face into his warm hand.

'I know I never will,' she said.

Their hands clasped and joined and their gaze locked on each other, ignoring the noise and celebration around them.

There, in their joined hands. There it was, that sense of home she'd been searching for all her life. Home, and love, and peace, and desire. All she'd ever wanted, and more than she'd ever dreamed of.

As though he'd heard her thoughts, Endellion said, 'We'll make our own family. Here, in Tanjore. A family full of love and, and-'

'Tenderness. Tenderness and safety and belonging.'

His eyes misted. How strange it was. Their lives couldn't have been more different, but they both came to this moment with the same longings.

'Yes! Lots of children, and all of them loved.'

Her own eyes pricked with tears. It scarcely seemed possible, but here she was, in India, looking ahead to a life full of love and family.

'You'll be a wonderful mother.'

Sarah shook her head. That wasn't quite right.

'*We* will be wonderful parents.'

His whole face lit up; not just with love and happiness, but with glorious possibility.

'Yes.' He increased his grip on her hand, and glanced at the others, perhaps wondering if he was allowed to kiss her fingers. The princess glared at him, and Sarah laughed.

'Not long,' she said.

A wry smile twisted his mouth, but his expression changed into something more serious.

'And then we'll be together forever, and no one shall ever keep us apart.'

Yes. A thousand times yes!

'Together forever,' she said, and kissed him, not caring that the whole room gasped.

Together forever.

MORE BY ELIZABETH LEYDIN

I hope you've enjoyed the sixth book in the Trengrouse Ball series. There are more–see below.

Sign up for Elizabeth's Substack blog, 'Corsets & Coaches', where she shares true-life Regency stories and tidbits, as well as news about her latest releases, or watch her "This Week in the Regency" videos on Youtube.

More Trengrouse Ball Sweet Regency Romances

The Captain & The Lady
Book 1 in The Trengrouse Ball series

Petroc Trengrouse has come home from Waterloo missing his right leg. Family friend Lady Beatrice Marlowe has been thrown out of her home on the deaths of her father and brother.

When Petroc comes to stay at Beatrice's mother's seaside house to recover from his wounds, he has no idea that he's causing severe financial problems.

He feels he's not fit to marry; she knows she's too poor to attract an aristocratic suitor. Will the Trengrouse Ball prove both of them wrong?

The Youngest Son
Book 2 in the Trengrouse Ball series

A heart-warming, forced marriage friends-to-lovers romance.

When Ives Trengrouse hijacks his friend Den's coach after the Trengrouse Ball, he thinks it's no more than a prank. But Den isn't inside. Instead, it's his sister Katie, going home early with a migraine.

Compromised beyond saving, the two must marry immediately—and do so. Katie's dreams of a big London Season are gone. Ives can't go on his light-hearted, care-for-nothing way now he's a married man.

Neither of them wants to be in this marriage: can they turn childhood friendship into something deeper?

Second Chance at Christmas
Book 3 in the Trengrouse Ball series

A heart-warming second chance Christmas story.

Widowed, pregnant Lady Demelza Mandeville returns to her family home, Trengrouse Hall, after her husband's recent death, dreading meeting family friend, Sir Denzell Kelynack, who jilted her in her first Season.

Denzell looks forward to the meeting—he wants to know why Demelza had jilted him eight years ago. And what role did his needy, unstable mother play in that?

Finding out the truth, and finding a path to a new life, is complicated by Demelza's pregnancy. If the baby is a boy, she'll be bound to the Mandeville estates until he's an adult; if a girl, she's free to live her own life while a Mandeville cousin inherits the estate.

The Trengrouse Ball is a promise of things to come, but will the promise come true at Christmas?

The Baboon at the Ball
Book 4 in the Trengrouse Ball series

A forbidden love story with animal antics to upset the normal order of things! (Or, a Cinderella story with a difference...)

Val Muffet is a Cit—a rich, well-educated, beautifully-mannered man, but definitely *not* one of the *ton*, despite being invited to the Trengrouse Ball.

Lady Kerenza Trengrouse's family is amongst the great and the good of the land, and she expects to marry a lord. An earl, at least!

What could bring these two to care about each other? Enter Genevieve, the lost, forlorn but definitely challenging baboon, given to the Muffets by the Prince Regent himself.

Genevieve is *not* invited to the ball, but she comes anyway, and life will never be the same again for Val or Kerenza!

My Earl, the Spy
Book 5 in the Trengrouse Ball series

An exciting ace romance with a twist of espionage!

Lady Melissa Trengrouse can't imagine being married to anyone but Charles Goddard, Earl of Westholm, for whom she decodes secret French dispatches.

Although she hates the idea of marriage or children, for Charles, Melissa would endure it all. They're perfect for each other: but when she proposes to him at the Trengrouse Ball, he refuses her without explanation.

Charles has his reasons. He hates hurting her, but it's a relief when he has to ride off on a secret mission for the Crown.

Melissa realises he's riding into a trap. Can she save him and discover his secret reasons for denying that he loved her all along?

A sweet Regency romance with an atypical couple!

www.ingramcontent.com/pod-product-compliance
Lightning Source LLC
Chambersburg PA
CBHW070953180726
48291CB00004B/1267